BRIAN BOTTLE

JOHN GARTON

MONDAY night 30th October.

I'm on the third floor of a four-storey house. A double-bedroom, lounge through kitchen and bathroom, that's been modified and decorated by a variety of previous tenants. I can't afford the time or masses of spare cash to do much and why should I? My attitude being the same as any tenant before me therefore consigns me to exist between the African influence of a tenant long gone, and some kitsch retro hippies. Most recently streams of Indie-loving students and a smack head made their mark on the place. I know this having been periodically accosted outside by people looking for him... lucky me.

I grade mattresses in animals. The one I'm on has got to be twenty years old, and whereas it began life as a fleet... (is it a fleet?) ...of graceful swans, it has now turned, and has been turned many, many times into dead donkeys' hooves and ears. The least offensive ears are located near my head. The hooves are posthumously kicking shit out of my knees, hips, and elbows. Ultimately it's time to get another, or yet another night's sleep will result in a smashed back for me. Twenty years of blood, sweat, tears and God knows what else has gone into the making of this. It weighs a ton, but I guess that's the herd in there as well as all the dried fluids of man and womankind. I guess it's my main, and maybe only, incentive to get up in the dark autumn-cum-winter mornings. Dark when I scrape the frost and ice off my car window, and dark when I set off home again from work, finally parking it in its precarious place outside my flat.

My lounge-kitchen has a big window to look over a garden that belongs to us all, but really belongs to the winners in the basement and on the ground floor. I also look high enough over the street at the stuck-on net curtains of an unfrosted bathroom window that's occupied by two student nurses. This scene is replicated all the way down and into tens of other streets in this part of town. Welcome to a red brick world of Lego. A Minecraft-tinkle of breaking windows is the background music to the dance of kebab wrappers and junk-food boxes blowing serenely down an increasingly gusty road. Now and again small maelstroms catch up this trash and whirlpool and twist it into the paths of mountain-biking students, reminding me of past outdoor pursuits, but in far nicer surroundings.

This will all be behind me soon I convince myself, but who knows? The white freestanding oil filled radiator on castors is pretty much my only purchase to protect myself from the ravages of a cold winter ahead. Without this hundred-quid buy the flat would need scrapers to remove films of ice from the inside of the flat's windows.

The mattress is a double on a creaky-framed mélange of two by one. The only good news is that in recent times single occupants have left an almost body shaped dent in the centre. With three strategically placed pillows (my own, I'm not that trusting) I can cover myself with the duvet (mine too) and immerse myself in protection from the impending cold. The body dent allows me to remain relatively static, but with an adventurous toe I trace the rings of iron that are the springs, ominously close to breaking through and skewering me. I am still kicked to death by night, it's a lost situation any way you slice it.

I'm kind of in between girlfriends too at the moment. The last one left and took the huge, heavy blanket that acted as the United Nations buffer zone between the donkey hooves and us. When I say in between, I really mean one's gone and there isn't another. It's certainly minimalised the contents of the flat, and highlights some glaring deficiencies in the kitchen part of the lounge. No more microwave food for a while, and the flat's original toaster has come back onto the scene as Mr. Morphy Richards has left the building. Bitter? Me? No. Faultless? No. Philosophical? Getting there. It's under this cut-away scene that my night in a body shaped hole, protected from the world, is spent dreaming about Brian.

The dream probably has nothing to do with him. It's when you're still awake and kind of drifting that the images float in. I'm reminded, although I'm a bit young or maybe disinterested, of a sitcom from the 70's or 80's with that Ronnie Corbett. He was a librarian too and he always said sorry to his mum or something similar. I get a mental image of a very understated and elegant old-fashioned, wood-panelled hallway throwing a 1930's projection in my mind's eye. A shrill woman's voice shouting *Timothy!!* All this is going off in my head as I superimpose an image of a wheelchair and a librarian called Brian. The snail from the film The Magic Roundabout slithers into my head and as I make that leap into sleep, I knock a spring which goes boing and Zebedee tells me it's time for bed. I'm gone.

I wake up. It's Tuesday morning. Winter seems to have arrived a month early with a dark 7am. Upstairs are already rowing and I get the arse end of it. I don't get the rows anymore but pay double rent for the privilege. Before I go on I want to tell you what little I know about Brian and what I was doing in his life, or half-life.

MONDAY daytime.

I graduated as a mature (hah!) student from a poly in a northern city with a Desmond in Social Behaviour and Welfare Rights. Mature merely because my gap year had taken on a life of its own. It had benignly grown from the ski chalet chief cook and bottle washer, to the Greek islands transfer rep, back to the Alps as a sous, then on to Italy to chef; met a girl, travelled, came back, we fell out, met another girl at a party, too many parties; it became malignant.

I decided at last to do something with my life and applied to university, don't ask what I was doing on that course because I couldn't tell you and then decamped to Leeds on the offer of a job in this multi-agency task-force. A holistically approached social care programme, or at least their job spec said so, and my creatively written C.V. mirrored exactly. Prior to all this, my "proper" job was actually as an estate/property manager for a huge letting agency, which sat bizarrely well with said job spec. After a series of interview panels I probationed for three months, followed social workers around, learned how to lift someone out of danger, how to actually lift someone (not with my back) or know when to call a lift team; mix that with workshops from Care in the Community and Care at Home, getting to grips with social standards and welfare committees plus anything else the agency deemed fit.

Finally getting to grips with psychological report writing, requesting sensitive data protected information, and submitting complete case notes and recommendations I end up as one of their new, and I mean new, care assessors; this is a pilot scheme. We do well here and we roll out to the Midlands and then the rest of the country.

Anyway I have a real sense of pride that I will be at the forefront of this service and I guess with the help of supervisors and case study meetings, and obviously my outrageously extensive experience and knowledge of all things social (not) I'm unleashed on Brian. I don't know who'll feel worse, him or me. Mind you, on being given his case notes, a small stack, and seeing him in six close-up colour hospital photos, I'd probably hazard a guess and say him.

It's a holistic approach, y'know, the whole process. *Look at the whole*, I think as I look at the hole in the side of his head, 'I have to see a solution to your entire problem.' Think of a black hole in deep space sucking everything in. Nothing comes out. Apart from a glint in the eye: which could just be a reflection of the overhead hospital ward strip-light. This guy has been in one hell of an accident. I face the human equivalent of a black hole. Cold as it is, I perceptibly feel a downward movement in temperature.

We're in the occasional conference room, all of us, Director, Line Managers, Assessors, auxiliary staff, about a dozen of us altogether. Later the press will be given publicity packs about the flagship initiative. For now we're sitting in the conference room flicking through the additional paperwork we have on top of our own individual cases.

One of the more ludicrous acronyms we've developed in our new unit is CRASH. It stands for Cost, Rehabilitation, Action, Society and Holistic. It is a bag of shite. The cost, first on the list should actually be the last because well, it's all the money required for the R, A and S that equal cost. The holistic babble was thrown on by the corduroy-jacketed Director of Social Services to form this inappropriate, but pretty fair word, as far as Brian is concerned.

We're all nodding off listening to the Director when bizarrely, in the team pep talk, he says that now RoSPA has been unshackled somewhat from the European hymn sheet they are now pressing for BST to be scrapped. Someone asks what BST stands for and someone behind me says,

'It's a TLA.'

Silence brings, 'What's one of them?' to the response,

'Three Letter Acronym.'

Once this has settled down, a slightly irate Director reasonably tells the room that driving to work in the morning is generally seen to be safer than the return journey after work. Simply put, your morning commute is relatively unchanging whereas the homeward journey often includes late variations, sudden stops at the chip shop/Chinese takeaway, picking up the milk and suchlike. Ergo, more evening accidents than morning ones. If there was an extra hour of light, the argument goes, we would be more aware of other road users. This would result in fewer accidents and case-loads to deal with as we wouldn't have as many damaged lives in which to intervene.

'This,' the Director says 'may not in itself be of relevance to what we do but should be in all that we consider. The country, according to the Government, must see itself, rightly or not, as a whole. We owe it to our casework to wholly fulfil our obligations. Now, go forth.'

'We followed what the Germans were doing in 1916,' says a voice from the back, 'banged an extra hour on for the war effort.'

The Director doesn't respond, picks up his sheaf of papers from the desk and walks out. Everyone relaxes.

I'm sure there's a failure on our part, or more specifically on said Director, to actually introduce our unit formally to all the agencies we may need to deal with. I suspect too that there's some political dimension to this but hey ho. The file I hold, though thrown together, has ultimately come from our unit. No ISO accreditation for this one.

So, Brian. I hold his notes - address, date of birth, next of kin and occupation, amongst others. I scan this and find his folks are dead, his occupation is ex-librarian, ex as in recently made redundant. It's a bit half assed on my part but I'm gathering my thoughts and trying to do this right. I flick through some of my own hand written notes from the unit and see that the Criminal Injuries Compensation Authority suggest seventy quid per stitch, I'm sure I've messed up here and it should be seven hundred. Mental note to check later. I've been presented with this file, cobbled together by too few people who don't really know, care or aren't fully aware of our remit. Its incoherency in chronology means me chugging through different agencies' knowledge of Brian, that includes DSS history (none), his very recent hospital and doctors' reports (road traffic accident), employment records (library service), domestic details (none), electoral registration (yes), credit history (irrelevant), criminal record (no). That's the gist of it. This is for me to read and digest.

My job then is to assess, through this information, how much effort it's going to require to rehabilitate, take action, and involve society in a holistic solution. That spells RASH. I said it was shite. Cost shouldn't come into it, because my job is to assess his needs, not work out the price he might ending up paying. Shouldn't any money coming his way just be his for being half-killed?

Anyway, true to the remit of my job spec what I'm actually going to do is read up as much as I can and glean from the information I have how much is coming Brian's way, if any. From that limited information I'm going to try and work out the whole picture. Does he have any dependants, neighbours, friends who can help? What sort of state are his affairs in? We do actually care because we want him to be dropped back into planet world. We want him to lead a life, albeit somewhat altered, but better than an institutionalised one, unless, and this is the rub: if the cost to us, you and I, is less to have him in an institution. Then he doesn't make it back to planet world. If it's less to have him in his modified world he goes home. Not exactly socialism at its best but a win/win all round, especially as I'm led to believe that there's a massive insurance claim to be added to this recipe.

I decide to meet him properly tomorrow. I don't have a deadline as such with this but my immediate supervisor Maureen, we all call her Mo, wants a case study meeting in two days. That gives me tonight to gen up on a case, a man, I will always know as Brian Bottle, ex-librarian. I'll chat to him tomorrow... although his interim carer said that wouldn't be possible... well I'll speak to the carer instead. Then over to the case study meeting where I'll hand over the file for the next assembly line process. Having worked here and there over the last few years I'm not convinced about this two-day job, done and dusted, away you go. I just feel that it isn't enough time. Just as I'm closing the file I notice the medical statement showing Brian had 120 stitches from the edge of his nose and going pretty much over the top and down the back of his ear to his neck. At seventy quid a pop that's quite a slice but if it's seven hundred he's quids in. The law changes, I think, to a half million maximum. Nevertheless, if there's insurance on top hopefully we can get our boy back to Earth.

I struggle in traffic, leapfrogging the packed student buses down Headingley Lane and head into red brick land. There are lights on everywhere as students burn electricity, pasta and rice, the windows a mass of condensation. The two nurses must be getting ready to go to work as one of them runs into the un-opaque lounge window in a black bra. I know you can't see her from the ground floor in the bathroom window but seemingly I can from my room. Heaven knows what the guy with the dormer window in the flat above gets to gawp at. I throw the Polo into a slot, wheel lock it and push down the aerial. I'm startled by a bang, then another and remember it's coming up to bonfire night. In reality it's not 'til next month but the shops have been selling fireworks for weeks now. Thinking ahead to my future caseload, it'll probably include an eight-year-old boy hit by a thrown firework, losing two fingers. I'll collate all the agency reports and the CICA will give him three grand a finger. I don't honestly know, they change the criteria most years and I could be three or four years in the wrong. Six gee's and Bob's your uncle.

I get in and make myself beans on toast under a smallish grill, with some grated cheddar on top. Eating it is no more interesting than making it and outside I can hear the muffled krumphs as bangers are let off. Setting aside my food I pick up my blue case folder and look for any recent Census data or family history and come upon a sheet of A4, probably typed by Geraldine from the office.

It's a jumble of dates and names in no particular order starting with Brian's birth in August 1981. Grabbing a blank A4 sheet I start to pen a more coherent timeline, remembering my course tutor's insistence on painting a picture. Time and place, time and place.

I go no further back than his parents starting with:

Norman Albert Ball b.15.2.1928, m. 04.1956, d. 3.6.2004 aged 76.

Dorothy Agnes Verity b. 20.03.1936, m. 04.1956, d. 10.11.2016 aged 80.

Donald Ball b. 08.02.1960.

Brian Norman Ball b. 25.05.1981.

Norman marries Dorothy 1956. He's 29, she's 21.

So, Brian has a much older brother about whom we know what? When he was born the dad would have been 31 and Dorothy 23. Then along pops Brian to a 53 year old man and 45 year old woman. Some surprise!

The noises outside have ramped up; sirens and bangers, rockets coming down the back alleys. This is the next week's soundtrack for everyone around here and quite a frightening one for some residents; but in a spirit of not being defeated I make my way to the local pub and stay there 'til kicking out time, chewing the cud with some kids who live a couple of doors up from me. The tunes are drowning out any useful talk and I remember the tunes from not so long ago, pretty much the same as these. It feels like change doesn't change much, or fast, unless it's a change for the worse. Sticky carpets in pubs never change.

A bit wobbly when I get back so I don't read anymore about my man, but the little I do know has obviously disturbed my thought pattern. As I drift into my cocoon mattress and start dozing I'm dreaming about Brian Bottle.

TUESDAY 31st October.

First thing after I get up and dressed in the cold, and peace now that upstairs have stopped arguing, is make a decision to go into the office and see Mo. I postpone seeing Brian until Wednesday because frankly he isn't going anywhere soon. It's not that I'm over-awed by the task, though I know it's a bit more of a challenge than the one I was spoon-fed. No, I want to see her and try to understand a bit more what I need to do. I explain that the files are not really up to scratch, which results in a semi roasting for Geraldine, who put this file together. I didn't intend that and I'm shot nasty looks for most of the morning. Mo sits me down with the file and we discuss what I'm hoping to achieve with this case.

'I want to get more info on the guy,' I start. Mo nods. 'I mean, his head's kinda caved in.' Mo doesn't nod. 'I don't mean to sound flippant Mo, but seeing his file and notes yesterday I just felt totally unprepared, there's loads of stuff missing that I'm sure would relate to this.' More nodding. '…and my gut feeling right now would be that he's not going to rehabilitate in his present state.'

Mo is surprisingly sympathetic and tells me that this is a new era in social care.

'Our older methods of social care have become almost extinct and it's an evolutionary process we're going through.'

You know when you can tell someone is lying? Mo isn't lying but isn't telling the truth either, this is more like a half-truth. Three years of university; she can't tell me that everything I learnt is suddenly dust!

Mo adds that Social Services hold a set of keys somewhere for Brian's house, and says it might be a good idea to visit his home. Use official guidelines and protocols for staff working in other people's homes and basically case the joint. She slides the key release request form across the desk to me,

'…work out what modifications would need to be made to

convert his home so he can live there. See if any of his neighbours have anything that will ultimately help us in our assessment. This is where the good old fashioned practices of social services, but remember old-fashioned, Simon, are married to our new vision for this provision.'

Am I being schooled here? Mo is telling me one thing but seems to be saying the opposite. She's smiling and I can see she's getting well into the rhetoric, but it's taking me away from what I came in for. I wanted order, a timetable, an A to Z guide. Luckily she back pedals and says,

'But to do this you need to establish what his capabilities are. To do that you need to read his hospital report and the reports of the interim care worker and actually speak to...' she looks down, 'the patient... no, Simon I didn't mean to say patient but I can't think what to call ermm... Mr. Ball.'

Finally, she postpones the case review meeting for a week. This, she says will give me a few mornings to come in and re-collate all the information, find out what's missing, gather that. The rest of the time will be spent assessing the reports and then visiting Brian, his home, his neighbours, his family if he has any, his ex-colleagues. I know all this, it's what's been on my mind. What I need is guidance. Mo chucks in that I need to hit the ground running on this as more casework will be along soon.

'We're all a little - a lot, under the spotlight,' she's giving me the closing speech, 'and it really is in the interests of the unit that these new cases are dealt with to the best of our abilities. All we do in these endeavours is gently allow change now to develop our strategy for future change. Some old practices coupled with new ones that we've yet to see, but will come to fruition...'

My eyes are glazing over and I wonder if Mo and I will reach that climax together when both parties realise one has lost the plot and is talking shit. A small sigh indicates we have. Mo is staring into nowhere when suddenly her shoulders prick to attention. She looks at me with *I've just overcome Alzheimers* eyes and tells me that Brian isn't our patient, no, he's our client. Over her shoulder on the wall is a laminated sheet of A4 with three sentences:

Don't say it doesn't – it does!

Don't say it wouldn't – it would!

Don't say it can't – it can!

I don't like its apocryphal stance, especially in this job. The amount of case studies I've seen with those immortal words, that window *doesn't* open out that way, my dog *wouldn't* bite, that fire *can't* be switched on by a toddler. A shudder goes through me.

I leave our office, walking past the transport department, the sports for schools department, the photocopier where Geraldine is still giving it the daggers. I have a key release request form that I take to the Social Services department a floor above and I collect the keys for 29 Upper Park Crescent.

TUESDAY lunchtime.

Outside, lunchtime-ish and I pull out of the car park and drive into Headingley for a sandwich. Tuna and cucumber is the closest I get to a real one, though it's on brown in a plastic triangle box. It's thrown onto the passenger seat and I'm going home, slowly, there's no rush hour in this part of town, not even at lunchtime. Peeling the lid back I start on my sandwich between stops and starts. No tram system in place but I'm not sure that would solve this issue anyway. The traffic seems to always be heavy, day, night, morning, evening. A labouring, polluting artery. The traffic slowly flowing through town to the city centre and the sandwich gone long before my turn-off.

Being afternoon though, I get a good parking space right outside my house. I look across the bonnet and see that my aerial has been snapped off and groan, that really has emptied any joy out of the day. I look again and realise that I hadn't, in fact, pulled it out from last time. My quality of life ratchets back to where it stood twenty seconds ago. Such are the frailties I endure at the moment. I notice then that I hadn't even had a tape playing or the radio on today, and feel that I've missed out on something that might have shaken the world.

I go up to my multi-cultural flat, passing those lucky people on the ground floor. Tim, I think he's called, tells me that they're having a party on Saturday with fireworks in the garden, and hopes I understand if there's a bit of noise and that it might go on late. As a social faux-pas is about to be committed he throws in the obligatory,

'Are you gonna come? You're welcome to, it starts about ten?'

I answer in the affirmative with the rider that if I end up doing something else, I won't. I get in and the flat is warm. The watery sun has been drifting on its arc through the lounge/kitchen. I switch the radio on, rolling news, nothing of any note has happened; I make a coffee, sit down and read the files properly. I finally complete reading his file in amongst a few goes on Cubescape on my phone, and notice the dark outside has been relentless. It's taken me three hours I calculate (in truth probably half an hour) to get a picture of the man I'm here to help.

Starving now, I put on a pan of water and slip a boil-in-the-bag Cod-in-Parsley Sauce in. In the same pan new potatoes from a tin and some frozen spinach make up my tea. *I'm better at this*, I say to myself looking at the awful food I've taken to eating. Memo to self: must try harder. Whilst this is cooking I try the same level of Cubescape that I've been stuck on for at least a week and start pondering the shit and turmoil I've had in my personal life lately. I feel a twinge of something that's either guilt or pity when I look at how quickly Brian's life has utterly collapsed. I realise I've been stuck for months.

What is it they say? Well it's what Mo said,

'Have some sympathy with this one, walk a mile in his shoes.'

A fucking mile, I wouldn't even put his shoes on. Has Mo mistaken sympathy with empathy? Nevertheless the response would be the same.

'Have some empathy with this one; spend an hour in his head.'

Again thanks for the offer, thanks but no, thank you, no.

All of his records formally name him Brian Norman Ball. To me he will always be Brian Bottle.

WEDNESDAY 1st November.

The next morning, a new month, I grab a shower, shave, put on some work trousers and a shirt and jumper and grab a coffee. I phone Mo from my mobile and leave a message on voicemail telling her that I'm seeing Brian's interim care worker this morning. Then I phone the home again and tell them I'll be along at ten.

That's the big problem when operating pilot schemes. There are a dozen committees waiting for the pilot to work before they'll throw any money at it. This means that I use my own car, my own smart phone, my own laptop and a shared pool tablet. We haven't even got office PCs just that shared handful of laptops to play on. The office is a transitional space while we prove our worth and share our desks. For sure all the work calls are reimbursed as is the wear and tear on my car, but it's kind of on the wrong footing to start with. I'm half glad that this particular case has dragged through to another week just so I can be thorough enough to show that the right decisions were made for Brian. Plus I've avoided the possibility of going to some fingerless kid's house.

Brian, I presume, is sitting in a wheelchair in the patients' lounge when I get to the halfway house/interim care home. His back is to me and I follow his sightline to a squirrel tear-arsing up the trees in this walled-off garden. Are nut-gathering techniques an avenue down which his mind can even wander or wheel? He's mumbling something to himself and I can just about hear him repeating his name. He's trying to vocalise the Brian but not doing so great and when saying Ball he stops and starts almost immediately. I've found that Yorkshire people do this with words like butter, cattle and metal where the letter t is unheard. Brian stumbling over the word Ball makes it sound like bottle but without pronouncing the t.

A voice behind me says,

'Hi, I'm Tim.'

I turn and meet another Tim. This one is half a head taller than me and is dressed as though he's about to go to the gym. I imagine that lugging great lumps of patient, sorry client, around requires a certain degree of athleticism. He offers me a coffee, which I take him up on.

'Milk and one,' I call out as I'm left stranded. I follow Tim to a user-friendly, neat and tidy kitchen. I haven't even introduced myself and don't get the chance now as Tim asks,

'Your office called about Brian?'

'No, I did,' I say.

The time for introductions has passed on this occasion and I think, *whatever*. I remember the case under my arm and set it down on the dining table, open it and produce a clipboard and pad. I sit down and Tim brings two coffees to the table. He puts them down and then slings a hand out for me to shake. This is awkward as I'm sat down so I scrape the chair noisily back, stand, shake his hand and say,

'Hi I'm Simon. How is Brian getting on?'

My pen is poised for a marathon and Tim replies that he's okay.

'Can he get around?' I ask. Tim replies no. 'How long has he been in here now?' I'm waiting on a short answer and am given,

'A month.'

This is already very trying. I could, if I wished, carry on this virtual monologue with Tim but I realise this teeth-pulling exercise is benefiting no one and so I change tack and ask Tim how long he's worked here. I coax him to build a picture of this place, of the things that matter to the welfare of the clients. Tim is far better at this and starts by taking me on a guided tour and going through the facilities at the halfway house, coffee cup in tow. Non-slip dimpled ramps are dotted about the access doors of this purpose built single storey building, erected circa 1982. The corridor is high and airy with skylights splitting the building down the middle. Arriving at the warden's office there's a plaque on the wall confirming the mayor of 1981 laid the first stone.

'A lot of money got thrown at this area after the riots of '81, a life-time ago,' says Tim.

'It'd be nice if someone chucked some money our way,' I reply.

Tim nods and tells me he only knows this because of what other workers have passed on to him, since he's only been here three years.

We come to a largish dayroom and I count six chairs, seven

if you include Brian in his wheelchair, oblivious to Tim and me. There's a big canteen table that wouldn't look out of place in a university refectory, and a big new telly in the corner. A serving hatch draws me to the kitchen we've recently vacated.

'The last one got nicked five weeks ago,' adds Tim.

Not another serving hatch burglary?! I'm about to say when Tim walks into Brian's circle, or whatever shape, of vision he has and asks him in a friendly manner,

'Do you want the TV on?'

Brian doesn't respond, so Tim puts on the telly and puts the remote back on top of it. No point in me assaulting his senses any further, so I stay put until Tim comes back and we walk out of the lounge.

'Is Brian the only one here?' I ask.

'Yes,' replies Tim.

This is a bit unsettling and I'm about to question Tim further when he tells me that the other four are out for the day.

'They go out every Wednesday to a special day care unit where they have bingo and stuff. Brian's not up to it yet, probably another six weeks and he might be.'

'Six weeks,' I say, 'that'll be the Christmas bingo then?'

'I guess, if you say so,' replies Tim 'we try to have a client turnaround time of less than three months here so yeah, twelve weeks takes Brian to the New Year.'

'We'll have to crack on with his house,' I say.

'We'll have to get the physiotherapy ramped up to see if he can cope,' adds Tim.

'How many of these type of cases have you done, Tim?' I ask. His reply of 'that'll be none,' releases a laugh from me.

Tim goes on to explain that he knows that the pilot scheme for this is here and is happening now with Brian. His line manager has clued him up as far as she can and he is just waiting for me to take command, so to speak. Well at least the ice has been broken and any tension has gone. My being Commander-in-Chief is, however, another matter.

Past the kitchen again and we're at the cleaning cupboards and toilets, just off to the right is a room which I'm informed is the night staff's room and control centre if you like.

'Sometimes there's one on duty or sometimes two,' I'm told.

Down this side of the building are six further rooms, the bedrooms. There's another toilet at the end of there, and at the very bottom of the building is the warden's room, a sort of staff office. The shape of the building is rectangular with another bit stuck on at the end. It all looks pleasant enough, but has a forgotten feel to it, like it was new in the eighties but not much has been done since. I think it feels like a halfway house, transit land, anywhere station... my flat.

Later, about half an hour, fifteen minutes tops, I'm sitting with Tim, with another coffee and discussing Brian in more detail.

'Brian will need 24 hour, or what we call waking assistance for now,' says Tim. 'He's pretty immobile apart from his right arm below the elbow and his facial muscles have some movement. He's a little like a very severe stroke patient. There are some movements he can make that don't make much sense, like his arm only moving below the elbow and he may make a recovery but how well we don't know. You can never be too careful when it comes to head injuries.'

Tim has altogether got the hang of talking and I guiltily realise that he may not have too many conversational acrobats to whom he can chat during his day. I am listening, but feel I'll look to medical experts to tell me if the same symptoms apply.

'I've been trying to give Brian some vocal testing and there's some response there, though I'm not sure if it's cognitive or not,' says Tim.

If Tim's information is poor on Brian's condition then I've wasted time, so I push him for his take on the facilities. Tim looks at me. He's waiting for a question. I ask him a question, a general one because I haven't seen Brian's house yet. Tim has, which is a surprise at first, but not so surprising when he explains why. He tells me that he was the one who'd passed the keys on to us after he'd been to Brian's to make sure all the utilities were secured, like no taps left running for a month, or the central heating ramped up to the max, that sort of thing.

'Where would you start with modifying his house?' I begin.

'His doorways would need enlarging, downstairs at least,' Tim responds, he's off and running. 'Then there's the access to his home for the wheelchair. He won't be going anywhere but the carers may wheel him down the pub now and again. There'd be little point in altering the upstairs of the property, downstairs you'd have to put in a bathroom, possibly swap the upstairs for downstairs if you know what I mean and shove the bathroom in the kitchen and vice versa. That alone might cause some difficulty, though not for Brian,'

'What do you mean?' I ask.

'Well, whoever was on shift to look after Brian would need to use a bathroom and creeping downstairs might upset him, or them so basically his lounge would have to become his bedroom and care room and the kitchen would be his bathroom/wet room and physio-room. Upstairs would be the kitchen and a flat with its own toilet for his carer or team, he'd only have one carer during the night, normally.'

This is way too surreal and I can't stop myself asking my next question.

'So whoever became his carers would have shifts to sort out who slept what nights?' I half-ask. 'Would they share, y'know the same bed, or would they have one each?'

I'm leading up to a question about mattresses here and can't stop. There's no, no really none, no reason to try to find out whether they share the same mattress. This is in no way helpful to Brian and I'm starting to inwardly squirm with my own embarrassment as I'm full-steaming down this line of questioning.

'Do the care team share the same mattress, Tim?' There, it came out staccato, machine-gun rapid.

'Yes they would, we do here anyway. Depends on the number of rooms.' Tim deadpans me the answer and I've stopped myself from going any further. I think I'm nearly done here for the day but I tell Tim I want to come back in a couple of days to catch up. I want to have a look at Brian's house.

'Whenever you want,' Tim says, extending the invitation to an open one.

'Err, can I go and say hello to Brian before I leave?' I ask. So Tim introduces me formally to Brian. In the same friendly tone he tells him,

'Brian, this is Simon, he's from Social Services and he's going to be here to assess what we need to do to get you back to your house.' Very succinct and in a nutshell exactly what I'm here for, so I just say,

'Hi Brian, I'm a member of the CRASH team...' I stop and realise what a ridiculous statement that was. 'I'll be back in a couple of days to sit down and discuss the best way for making your house ready for you to go back. I have a set of keys to have a look round and see what needs rearranging.'

The response from Brian is almost like someone having a seizure. Tim places his arm across Brian to stop him falling forward.

'Unusual,' Tim says, 'he's not done that before.'

Tim doesn't take it any further than that but I know that's what someone who's about to kick off would do.

I make myself look into his eyes. He looks different to the hospital ward pictures I've seen; his hair is growing back and the stitches are out. His head shape is near normal apart from a small caldera where the damage to his eye socket took place. The fault lines on his skull, where the skin was pulled over and sewn back, look like tectonic plates after a quake. Two earth shattering events on one head.

The stare I get from Brian is one of a deeply injured and hopelessly damaged individual. This is also the stare of one very angry looking fucker. Before I look away I get a momentary glimpse of someone who's scared, and I have a feeling, and a strong one at that, that he doesn't want me near his house. I'm only aware of a very twisted pissed off feeling when I walk away and leave to go to the car park.

I've made it to lunchtime and as I get into my car I switch on my mobile. There's a message from Mo asking me to let her know how I've got on at the centre and saying that she expects to see me in the morning. Well, that's my afternoon taken care of. Same sandwich as yesterday but I hope on white, a survey of Brian's house, probably best to stick my head in at the office, home to type up the recommendations and then off to the pub for another fun-packed evening. A warning flag pops into my head to remind me to get a torch in case his lights aren't on. I've no idea where that came from but I guess it makes sense as he's been out of action for some time; an empty house, unpaid bill equals no electricity. I don't want to use my phone as a torch. My counter-argument kicks in that the utility company would seek out this information before disconnection. My counter-argument loses on the basis that our own databases don't communicate with each other in the council, so why the hell would anyone else communicate with us or ours. Then I remember Tim saying that it won't be under water or like the Sahara, but anyway, I don't think I'm looking forward to going to Brian's empty house on my own. I'll choose not to enter that on my report.

I hop out of the car and open the boot. Next to the spare petrol can and travel blanket I see a torch, just a rubber handled job, I estimate about four of those big batteries worth, but it clicks on and there's light. Birthday, Christmas or new car present, I don't know, though I didn't buy it. I close the boot, encase myself in the driver's seat and feel a drop of sweat escape my armpit and hit my side. The aerial is down, so hand forward and bend over to reach under the seat, and find an old tape. The car's tape cassette player is built in. This part of town I'm informed, is one of the most burgled in the city. Apart from the yellow wheel lock there's nothing on display. Any low-life can see that the tape player is built in. It's Wi-Fi and Bluetooth only these days and I have an ever-dwindling stock of tapes. Useless unless they become the next fashion revival.

I expect one of these days to discover that the wheel lock has been stolen, therefore not find it but rather a sugar hill of broken glass. My hand comes back from under the seat and the winner is The Fabulous Bindis. This was a gift, kind of. Actually, the result of the *'half of everything is mine unless it's shit, at which point I'll leave you to dispose of it'* reality of a break-up. The track playing is woeful. At the time I was enthusiastically told that the Bindis were from Bangalore and were influenced by the Indie scene, kind of Cornershop before Fat Boy Slim got to them. I am depressing myself with some mildly obsessive behaviour, the mattress in my life, my car fucking aerial. It's only lunch and I'm already looking for a remedy to this god-awful day. A night down the pub isn't the best solution, but I remember it's Wednesday: quiz night at the Park. I fast forward the cassette straight into trouble as I hear the overstretched tape start to chew up. I haul out the tape worm, about four feet long, from the machine, wrap it around the cassette and return it, not gently, to the car floor. Smiling, I set off.

Upper Park Crescent lies on the periphery of student land and even looks to have families here. The first half of the street consists of large Victorian terraces, big old Yorkshire stone dwellings. Enough estate agent boards tell me that the families are on the way out though and the developers are moving in. Time will see soon enough that the large-roomed family homes will become multiple occupancy shoeboxes. Nicely gnarled ash and elm trees line most of the street, and the leaves are nearly all off, past the romantic run through them stage and now at their brown mulching decomposing worst. It isn't raining but it feels like it should be; a fine mist exists, not threatened by this pitiful excuse for a sun that might have been better not putting in an appearance this morning. I pass number 17 and look for a space to pull in. An old red Renault pulls out and I assume its place. Being careful I lock the wheel and make sure the aerial is down, it is. I get out and clutch my clipboard under my arm before grabbing the torch from the boot. Looking at the Crescent I spot a laminated sheet on the nearest tree informing the world that this tree is an ash and advising how to be vigilant against the latest tree disease. It reminds me of when I was younger and Dutch elm disease broke out and I can almost see a moment when this row of magnificent trees are wiped out. Here one day and gone the next, how sad.

Checking for the keys, I trudge down the road. Curiously at number 27 the terraces stop. The even-numbered ones continue all the way along the road, but the odd-numbered ones have changed into a 1930's row. I guess you'd call them town houses. There are three to a block and Brian's is an end one. There's a garage built onto the side of the house with dark green wooden doors which pull open. There are two low metal gates which push forward onto the shortest drive I've ever seen. I make a mental note never to buy a property like this. I'm not even sure a decent sized modern car would make it to the garage. Separating the drive from the flagged path is a small patch of grass, which clearly hasn't seen too much in the way of gardening. On the other side of the path is a bigger piece of lawn that has befallen the same fate. The house is stone at the bottom and half pebble dashed. The windows are pretty close to original, well maintained compared to the garden. Looks like they were repainted this decade. The front door is white like the windows, the bull's eye window in the front door is unbroken, and hinges are still intact. Most of the houses around here have grilles on the front and back doors, the dealers have grilles around the soil downpipes to stop the drug squad sawing through them to catch toilet-flushed stashes. This street has largely escaped such adornments, another sign of families and not a transient population. Brian's house; empty for a month and not burgled; a nice result I think.

The key is a bit stiff but I open the door and have to push against the mound of pizza and fast-food menus. They spill over the welcome mat and I slide through. The light coming through is still plenty for me to take in the room and it's a little like I imagined. I flick a light switch on the wall and a light comes on. I turn it off again and make a note that it hasn't been disconnected in the connected/disconnected box on my form. Somewhere in the pile of post there may be a bill, and that's something I'll eventually have to sort out. The law says I can't, but the agency says I can. We have some old and obscure Power of Attorney legislation that allows us to notify and contact need-to-know people, Mo says.

The vestibule door opens into a lounge and through this I can make out a door to a kitchen, probably. It's clean but old fashioned; there's a dull-patterned brown carpet, not threadbare, beige wallpaper, again not bad, just tired. It gives me a feeling of an old neighbour's house when I was growing up, pouring the dregs of cold tea onto the carpet, *slekking dust* she said. I recall she'd been from Yorkshire somewhere. The carpet has those clear plastic mats on that protect against wear. This feels like a home that belonged to grandparents. I see an ageing telly, not a flat screen but the ones as deep as they are across. *What's on the box*? pops into my head and I can see why, the thing is a box. The box is in the corner with a layer of two month old dust on the top and the screen and there's a tiled fireplace on the opposite wall. A gas effect heater sits in the grate and I guess a combi-boiler sits behind it, an old one if the radiators on the wall are anything to go by. The windows are in good nick and there are locks on them and an old faded yellow neighbourhood watch sticker on one. I don't think the burglars had tried to get in because there's nothing really worth having. Even the metalwork for the pipes and boiler isn't attractive enough for the metal thieves to remove. Junkies or squatters were more in line for this. Even cuckoos would like this, the lower than low who find a house like this belonging to a vulnerable person and start it up as a drug den, mostly at the ignorance of the occupier. I don't think it likely but all options must be kept in view.

Anyway, back to the job in hand. An app I've got on my phone works out room specifications to be uploaded via GPS. I allow location and place my device on the floor in the middle of the lounge, tap start and stand well back.

'Light the blue touch-paper,' I say out loud 'and stand well back.'

I've specified only brick and stone to be pinged off. Everything else is invisible, if you see what I mean. The beauty here is that the app gives me a 3D blueprint of the room due to parameters that I put in, say fifteen by fifteen and four feet down by ten high. This covers the entire room side to side and top to bottom. It shows all the gaps and distances with window and door frames, breakfast alcoves, anything solid or missing if you see what I mean. I'll repeat this throughout the house and download the data to my laptop later. I'll physically measure the rooms too to show that my workings have been thorough for the benefit of any technophobes on the panel. My clipboard has on it an inventory form and I set about filling in the contents by room. Walking through to the kitchen it's the same story. Decent cupboards and work surfaces from the eighties. A table sits in the middle of the room with four chairs, no carpet but the old linoleum flooring in yellow. A back door well bolted. A small, what looks like a pantry, lies off the kitchen and I peer in. I'm a little surprised to see four boxes of lager and half a dozen two litre bottles of fluorescent blue cider.

I trudge upstairs to see two double bedrooms and a small box-room. Carpets are non-descript general domestic and the wallpaper is a painted Anaglypta. The bedrooms have double beds in them. Firm mattresses that would have cost a lot of money, pocket-sprung both of them, still firm enough to feel like a thoroughbred; and a wardrobe apiece. The box-room has a chest of drawers with a bong on it, a hash pipe and box of Rips *like, what the fuck?!* Oh - and a nice view over a small back garden, the vista extending to sloping, wet grey roofs across the city. *Could there be a lodger?* I set the GPS to overlap the rest of the rooms well into the eaves and wait for it to upload to the app. The bathroom is functional for me but that's it. I take a piss in the separate and quite tiny W.C. and then have to walk back to the bathroom to wash my hands, the water freezing. It's getting colder as the sun has started to call it a day and I feel the same. Mo will want me to provide her with my findings so I decide to have another look tomorrow. I know already that there's a lot of modification required and I'm thinking it's a no-no. Getting back into the car I drive the mile or so to Headingley and stop off on my way to the office to see Brian again. I said it'd be a couple of days but strike while the iron's hot so to speak. I've got to build a relationship and trust with Brian, my social work brain tells me.

Tim isn't there but another giant appears before me. The warm air hits me as he opens the door and I tell him who I am. He grunts as I walk down to the day room. It's bathed in a warm glow and the television seems to be occupying the four returned inhabitants in the room. Brian is sitting in a different spot but isn't overly involved with anything. I pop over and say,

'Hi Brian, it's Simon from earlier, you remember me?'

No response but his good eye peers at me, a bit rheumy and

a bit nasty.

'I've been to your house this afternoon and everything's alright, no break…' I stop. Like he needs to be bothered whether he's been burgled. 'I've measured all the rooms to form a scale plan of your house,' I say.

Boy, do I give him the jitters. Everything I bloody say seems to produce neurological thunderstorms in his head. *Am I being insensitive?*

'Brian, can I ask when your parents…' I stop, 'tell you what, I'll come back some other time okay?'

I drive to work and spend the remaining half-hour with Mo having a coffee. I tell her where I'm at and she doesn't drill me out or anything heavy but she does remind me that the caseloads will be coming thick and fast if this thing gets going properly. I ask what will happen if the thing falls apart but she says it won't, kind of don't even sweat it that we're in any danger.

'The country is on its knees,' she says, 'do you really think that this Government or anyone else has a clue about tackling long-term problems?'

I tend to agree with her and as we stand in the small kitchen area I look around and can't argue against that.

'Years ago I got into this career because I wanted to make lives better,' Mo goes on, 'I want to prescribe to my chronically asthmatic patient not some inhaler, but a new central heating system,' she says. I'm about to *what the fuck* when she explains the holistic thing again. 'I'll always be giving away inhalers unless I get

33

to the underlying problem. Get to there, and the problem and its genesis are eradicated. Do you see?'

I tell her I'm going back to Brian's again soon. I also tell her I'm going to investigate his place of work in the morning. She chides me, I think and says something about not going all detective on her. I leave the building and glance at Face Ache typing on my way out.

Back on my street I find a parking spot a few doors from my flat and walk back up the slight incline, passing students coming the other way. It's raining steadily now and I can think of nowhere else that looks as drab as this on an autumn evening. Getting into my flat does nothing to alleviate this feeling and I realise that I'm lonely. I think about giving my ex a call but immediately think – *bad idea*, so instead I set about fixing tea. Some music is starting up in a flat nearby and my mood improves slightly as I feel the flat warming up from the cooking on the hob. Pasta and chopped up sausages in a tomato sauce with grated parmesan on top. Always fucking grated cheese on top. I sit in front of the laptop and watch the local news and there's a piece from the fire service telling us all to be careful with sparklers and bangers. '*My bangers taste quite good,*' I say to the reporter. Some resident fills the next twenty seconds with a clip of her Yorkshire terrier actually shaking like a shiteing dog at the sound of fireworks.

This house is starting to come alive with people back from Uni and work and I force a voice in my head to tell me to get a grip and do something. First I get changed into my playing-out clothes - jeans, T-shirt, sporty denim jacket and boots. One thing that hasn't bothered me until just now is how Brian got his injuries. I figure it isn't my role as care assessor to even know this as it might detract from whatever care I'll push for him, but still I wonder who or what did this to him and how. I pick up the notes to read about his accident but there's nothing there. Am I being too Sherlock Holmes? In the end I read that he was working just down the road and as my remit is to see the big picture I decide that I'll make a start on that in the morning. Right now though, as the clock ticks round to eight-thirty, I want to go out and get leathered. I pop into the big student pub at the top of the hill and see that I've either missed the quiz or it hasn't begun yet; it's still five deep at the bar. Freshers' week seems to never end, I just get served in a corner of the bar as a group of people in a three-legged race pour in and ten minutes later pour out again. The music is fairly bouncing along and I see a couple of faces that I know and nod at them. One of them, long-haired John I think, but if it is he's now short-haired John, comes over and says that there's a party later and do I want to come? Noncommittally I say maybe, and realise, with some despair that I haven't even heard from my mates for a few weeks. This nails home the thought that I've gone and lost my mates along with my girlfriend. They were our collective friends, and now by whatever universal law applies I'm on the wrong side of that coin.

I need to go outside and get some air. I've just realised how small my world has become and it's making me claustrophobic. Outside I reach for my six inch plastic cigarette. I vape and have done for two or three years, but it's now just outside the pub that I realise I'm missing the company of others. A steady emission of tainted smoke mixes with my cherry blossom in the cold smoking shelter. It doesn't really break my mood and I look around at the students having a great time and foot-tapping and head-nodding to the latest tunes. This is where I was I think, not five years ago. Not in this bar, but one like it. I wonder if Brian ever came in here at all. It's fairly close to his house. Anyway, whilst I've been mulling shit over I've nipped back in and out for two or three refills and am getting tired. I have a quick look around for John but can't see him. I smile and head-nod with the music at an attractive group of girls standing by the door, slip out and go home.

One of my ever-shrinking number of friends, an American who I worked with in the Alps, sent me a link that I've saved for the first series of a, for now, US-only comedy. At the moment it's called *I Blame Terrence.* I take my shoes off, pull the small coffee table to within a few feet of the sofa I'm led on and dump everything on it, half drunkenly firing up the laptop.

I Blame Terrence Episode 1

The opening credits appear. A Cine film, all scratchy, shows a small kid with Buddy Holly glasses being chased by, one can only assume, bullies; running across a grassed yard with a sprinkler spraying water onto a creosote-painted fence. Clearly trying to depict small town America, the music starts, some weird robo-folk tune with the spliced axing riff from Radiohead. The credits continue with a fast forward through junior school, the boy is still running, being chased through to prep school, high school and coffee shops then white picket fences before juddering to a halt and the Cine reel rewinding back to the coffee shop. At this point three words appear as if branded onto the screen

I Hate Terrence.

Hate is then erased and the word Blame replaces it.

A town sign says Anniesburg, OR, Pop 12,454.

The blacktop rolls up to a small street with single storey shops on both sides and parking slots variously filled with sedans and the occasional older station wagon. The camera pans along the street before swinging left onto a tree-lined avenue, with drives leading to a mixture of single and double storey housing. Newspaper boy on a Chopper throwing rolled up papers onto the stoops and porches. You get the picture. The camera pans back to the local mart where a young man, maybe fifteen years old, gets out of the passenger side of a long yellow sedan. He leans over to kiss his mum and says,

'I'll make my own way home, Mom.'

'Are you sure honey? I can wait here for you,' she responds.

He looks around nervously and can see a group of older lads and lasses at the end of the strip. He swallows and says,

'I'll be ok, see you,' and pushes the door shut.

He's wearing a pair of beige flannels and some white deck shoes, a plain white granddad shirt with no collar, has mousey coloured hair and not quite pint bottle glasses but they're fairly thick. The whole opening scene evokes the early eighties. The youths at the end of the street look like high school jocks now, but are the high court senators and judges of the future with their cheerleading entourage. They don't look his way. Terrence doesn't exist to them unless it's to abuse. Resolutely the lad steps forward to the mart and pushes his way through the door.

The camera boom swings out across the street showing a couple of cars driving down the road. One's a duck-egg blue station wagon with rust beginning to give the car a patina, the other a white convertible going the other way, with what sounds like *Pearl's a Singer* coming from its radio.

The next scene shows the same youth standing outside looking absolutely bewildered and terrified clutching a bag, with a man pointing a Polaroid camera at him, snapping away, comedy hat with the word PRESS typed on card stuck in the sash. Another man, presumably the shop manager is pumping his arm in an overly vigorous hand-shake. The jocks and their entourage are clapping and whistling. The scene finishes with a scream and the camera shot pans out from an upwardly tilted-tonsilled-throat that belongs to Terrence. He's screaming as the shot pans out like the Earth app and continues until it shows the street, town, wispy clouds, the State of Oregon, the North American continent, clouds, the Earth, all the planets, the Milky Way, ad infinitum.

A new scene starts with a newspaper front page spiralling quickly and then stopping at a picture of Terrence with the store manager underneath the headline *Super Kid Kingmaker*. It transpires that Terrence went into the shop to buy a record, that's all. Only, the record he bought had been number two in the Billboard top 100 chart and became number one solely on his one purchase, the week of Thanksgiving. It sounds innocuous but in the days back then it was a massive deal. Terrence therefore, mild and unassuming, becomes the hottest property of that week. More so even than the band he propelled into top slot.

The rest of the half hour long episode is spent showing a cartoon map of the States with planes setting off from all major airports and landing at Anniesburg's tiny airstrip, with comedy brake squealing. Fleets of cars are racing down the street where a man sign-writing the population figure keeps sighing and rewriting the figure: currently 13,989 and rising.

Next scene: Terrence being pursued by every marketing executive and advertiser worth their salt in America calling out,

'What brand shoes do you wear, Terrence?'

'What's your favourite drink/meal/band/ (insert any and everything)?'

Terrence, legging it through the meadow thinking this was the last thing on earth that he would ever wish for. Trapped and wondering how his world could get any worse. The music to this scene is Don't Fear the Reaper by Blue Oyster Cult and at the moment when the guitar solo screams in, Terrence is head in hands, almost moshing against a tree with his body.

His last thought before the credits roll is that if he's destined to live through Hell on Earth then so is everybody else.

It finishes with a sweating Terrence leaning against a tree, still in his thick glasses, granddad shirt, slacks and deck shoes. And yes, you have to think that Terrence is to blame for what follows. More robo-folk, the credits say music by Data Fig Shampoo whatever the shit that is.

Time to sleep. I pull the duvet back, lay the travel blanket from the boot of my car across the valley in the middle of the mattress and get in.

THURSDAY 2nd November.

Nine a.m. and the sun is shining weakly but at least it's the sun and everyone seems in a good mood. Nods and hellos from people on the street as I get into my car. The seat is warm already and I reach under it to try my lucky dip selection. The cassette in a clear box gives me no indication as to what it is but as I slip it in the opening beats to Sonnet – The Verve come through. This is the start of the weekend, I think to myself and pull away from the kerb. One of the nurses comes out of the door and waves at me. Have I won the lottery or something!? I get through the mile or so of traffic and pull up in the car park of the library. It's empty save for a black roadster. The library is just opening and an old lady is waiting at the door with a hessian shopping bag. I push open the door for her and get a *'ta love'*. While she's returning her books I wander over to the shelves and have a look at the hardbacks, new and clean, reference books and fiction all neatly boxed off. The old lady done, I remember that nobody knows I'm coming so I walk up to the wooden counter and clear my throat to the woman at the desk.

'Excuse me but I wonder if you can help me?' I ask.

'Yes love,' she replies 'are you a member or do you wish to join?'

She looks like she should be something else, not your

stereotypical librarian, and I wonder if she drives the sports car outside.

'My name is Simon, err… hang on,' I say as I reach into my pocket and pass over my card. Not really a business card and not really ID, this is something the agency's I.T helper knocked up for all of us a few weeks ago. It's the first one I've used. 'I want to speak to someone about Brian Bottle.'

'Sorry?' She looks at me a bit funny and I stand there like a lemon for a minute. She has a look that makes me think I'd last two minutes in bed with her.

'No, I'm sorry, I mean Brian Ball.'

'Are you the pol…?' she starts to ask, but then looks down at the card I've given her, and finally says, 'the poor man.'

'Yes.' It's all I can say.

'Sandra," she calls out softly, 'look after the counter for a while.'

A schoolmistress type click clicks her heels on the polished wooden floor towards us and the librarian whose nametag I just read as Miss Reid, *'Do not misread my name'* I almost say out loud but stop myself, says 'Follow me.' *Yes please* I think to myself.

We go into this room that's a kitchen cum lounge, a tiny version of the staff room at my old school. Miss Reid offers me a brew as she gets to the kettle and I say milk and one of whatever she's having. A couple of minutes later we're sat opposite each other holding mugs of tea, in those types of chairs from the sixth form common room that turn you into a cushion sandwich if you take the middle straps out. She looks about forty but that's deceiving, in a nice way. She actually looks like some of my old mates' mums from school, yes that good.

'What can I do for you?' she asks with the emphasis on I. Good start!

'I actually want some background information on Brian, err... Miss Reid.'

'Please, call me Helen,' she says with a warm smile.

'I'm his, Brian's, caseworker and I've just gone through his file. To help me build a picture of what the agency needs to do for him I just want some information, anything you can provide me with.' I'd prepared a list of questions in my head of what we might need and fire away, asking her whether she knew him outside of work, how long he'd worked there, whether she knew anything about his parents, what his specific job was and whether he had any prospects for work after redundancy. This sparks a question I hadn't written down about why he'd been made redundant in the first place.

'We'll use all this when we make recommendations for his future welfare,' I add. 'It's difficult for me at the moment because Brian isn't exactly telling us much about these things and the sooner he's rehabilitated the better for him.'

'I understand,' Helen says. 'Firstly, Brian was a valued member of staff here but as you may not be aware we're facing staff cut-backs. Well everyone is facing cuts aren't they?'

This sentence hangs in the air for a few seconds before she says, 'Did you know that you don't even ever need to come into a library anymore? You get your tab at home and join the library's on-line service and all the books we have are available for free. Where the hell will that leave the staff in the future? My team have got bloody degrees in library management.' It hangs there.

'Did Brian have a degree?' I ask.

'No, Brian started as a library assistant and then took the vocational in-work training; look this isn't the British Library, you know. These staff I have are thousands of pounds in debt and need the work. Brian's role is disappearing, he's got his own house and an inheritance. He's getting three months pay in lieu of notice and a redundancy figure you wouldn't sniff at.' She stops and it seems as though she's about to cry.

I see what's done this, the protection of her library family against a seemingly overwhelming force of the future.

'Poor man,' she says again. 'Brian, did I know him outside of work? Not really, or at least not until quite recently. One of the things that we did have was a support group going for the people whose jobs were under threat. The union suggested that it might be a good way to offer some relief from the stress that this shake-up had put us all under. And of course with Brian that stress was on top of him having just lost his mother.'

'When was this?' I ask.

'Not long ago at all. I think Brian's mum died at the start of the year...'

'What about his father?' I push.

'A good few years ago. Brian lived with them.'

'Did he live on his own after they died then?'

'As far as I know.'

'What was his job here?' I ask.

'Brian was our mobile librarian.'

'You mean the bus type library?'

'Yes he had a round that he would do five mornings and two afternoons a week for… oh, eleven years? He'd already been here for two years when the driving position came up. He was an extremely quiet man but well liked and reliable. Over the last few years though the demand for the service had dropped off and Brian was doing just two mornings and one afternoon when the threat of redundancies came up.'

'When was that exactly?' I ask.

'The union representative came to see all of us at the end of June,' she said. I picture myself with a pen rewriting the description of Brian's job in his notes from *Ex-librarian* to *Ex-mobile-mobile librarian* - can't work and can't walk. I smile stupidly; she's lifted her cup to her lips and that had pulled her breast up nice and tight. *Stop it* I tell myself, there's something more at stake here than a bit of titillation.

'So was this when the support group started?' I ask.

'Yes.'

'And what form of support was there, like regular meetings?' I intimate.

'Oh yes, in fact even though we've all been re-allocated our posts we still meet up,' she said and stood up as though my audience was over.

'Err… how many people work here now, then?'

'Four, now that Brian's role is being made redundant. You've met Sandra my deputy librarian, Susan is a graduate trainee and then there's Nadine who's a bit of an all-rounder.'

Helen walks over to the small metal sink where she sets down her cup and turns just in time to see me ogling her legs which are kept in place with some knee length black boots, more bedroom attire than library.

'Do you meet locally? This group?' I ask, quickly getting my last questions away.

'Yes, in the *Frame and Painter*,' she replies with nearly a wink, nearly a twinge, 'on a Wednesday after work.'

'Sorry," I say, 'do you know if Brian socialised outside of this support group?'

'Not that I know of, he was… is, a very, very quiet man who kept himself to himself,' she says.

'Perfect job,' I say. She's opening the door and I'm being invited to squeeze past her, which I start to do.

'Look,' she says 'Brian was what I'd call a non-drinker. He said he did drink but I got the impression he meant he had a glass of sherry with his Christmas dinner. I don't recall ever hearing him say he'd been out for beers.' She went on,

'The first time we all went out I had to personally shoehorn him into a taxi and he'd only had a couple of lagers.' She says this to me like she could pace herself for some marathon Friday night sessions. Not something I'd imagine myself doing anytime soon.

'One last thing. Had you noticed any changes in him recently?' I ask. Who did I think I was? Less Sherlock, more Columbo?

'Look,' she says, more coldly 'Brian's being made redundant. Over the last few months, what with his mum dying he's had some time off, which I put up with. I can't help that now and I'm sorry and I hope whoever did this, and yes we've all heard names, gets put away for a long time.'

Before I can even respond to her last sentence I'm ushered out and back to my car. As I'm about to pull out I see, parked up against the library, its mobile version. I get out for a look. I've never been in one and never seen into one and am curious as to how everything fits. It's smaller on the outside than I imagined but looking through the driver's window I can see that the passenger seat turns to face the customers. The bookshelves are built in a way that means they won't empty on bad corners, a set of steps are fastened to the end shelf with a bungee cord, and there's a big opening sky light that lets in loads of outside light. There's an empty computer table and a fabric skirt running around the bottom of the lowest shelf, security I guess to keep the valuables out of sight. A large drawbridge structure looks as though it's been added to the interior at a later date and, together with green and red buttons, composes the ramp for wheelchair access. Would Brian get to use this in his new capacity? A neat structure and a nice quiet job I thought.

Two questions I can't get out of my head as I drive to Brian's are firstly how come, if he didn't socialise and is this, in the words of his ex-boss, 'quiet man', he has loads of beer and cider at his house and also a bong and hash pipe? Could it be that someone else was living there? And the more pressing question now is who did this to him? I pull up outside number 29 and make my way to the door, opening it. Only two fast food menus had arrived since the day before. We usually got four or five a day.

The house is bathed in a warm light from the sun as it hasn't got to midday yet and I quickly set to work with the tape measure. Starting at the bottom, I measure the door jambs and then measure the distance wall to wall of the lounge and kitchen. The kitchen will need to be converted into both a physio-room and a shower toilet for Brian. This will leave his lounge as a bedroom as well. The layout isn't great and looking out of the window, the access to the front gate and garden isn't good. Finally I go up the stairs to measure the potential staff quarters. When the measuring and note taking is done I have a look at the finished plans and am pretty impressed with my effort. This is one of the centre-points of my presentation in that it will provide a quantity surveyor or building consultant with a rough idea as to costings. In the room that was obviously his mum's there is nothing other than a bed and built-in wardrobe and airing cupboard. I open it and there is I guess bedding, neatly boxed up and sealed, because the box has BEDDING written on it. There's no evidence at all of any occupancy. In what is obviously Brian's room there is bedding. It's neat and tidy and betrays nothing apart from when I go around the bed and find an overflowing ashtray on the carpet. This just puzzles me. Who was, or is, staying here? I finally go into the third room, a box-room you'd call it, and see a chest of drawers. I open the top drawer and pick up the notebook lying inside. It looks like the ones from school, dull orange cover, lined pages inside. I flick through the book and see it's nearly full with all-sorts. What looks like poems or song lyrics, maps, plans, recipes, letters to people, everything. I put it down on the top of the chest and open the second drawer and find this has more of the same exercise books, each one that I pick up, full. Stopping randomly at one page I notice a date from 26 years ago written in the margin. Another book I pick up has no dates. Another one is sixteen years old according to the date on one page. Is this his diary? His scrap book? A handful of stuff from newspapers and the NME? I fumble about in my back pocket for my phone and start to call Mo.

Ten minutes later I'm putting Brian's stuff into a black bin-liner and into the boot of my Polo. Mo doesn't want to see the books, enough on her plate already but she's given me permission to read them to see if they throw up anything useful, like relatives. I have to send her a completed form saying that I have the material and that I'm only going to read it for the benefit of the client and won't use it in any other way. Mo is quite adamant that I fully disclose to her that I have the material but at the same time tells me that I don't admit to anyone that I have the material. The minefield that is data protection and GDPR. Yeah Mo, like I haven't got loads of better things to do than read old schoolbooks. At the sound of my resistance Mo suggests I do it at home, in other words skive off at lunch and see you later, it's a deal.

I have to inventory his house at some point. I note he has a microwave but don't take it, I'm not like that.

As I'm leaving the garden this kid on a bike crashes into my leg.

'Watch where you're going!' I shout, to be met with,

'I'll sue you for damages.' He must be about eleven years old. 'What are you effing doing anyway? Are you selling the soldier's house?'

'The what? Whose house?' I ask.

'That,' says the boy, pointing where I'd come from 'is the ghost soldiers house.'

'Wait a minute, do you live round here?' I ask pointlessly, as he clearly does.

'Fuck off yer nonce,' he laughs and pedals off. He gets about ten doors down when out of a house opposite storms his mother. I start walking toward the pair who are now at raised voices level.

'Get inside,' she shouts before turning, surprised at my sudden arrival.

'I din't do owt,' the boy shouts back, dropping the bike on the path and slamming the door hard.

'And what do you want?' asks this weary lady 'are they selling the place? More student accommodation?' said sarcastically.

'Err... no, I'm not an estate agent,' I say apologetically and there's relief in her eyes, 'I'm from the Social Serv....'

Eyes slammed shuttered shut. Christ, how can I be lower than an estate agent?! Then I think truancy, fines for the kid not being in school, quick *re-rewind when the crowd say Bo Selecta* and placatory arm waving.

'Madam, I'll start again. I'm surveying number 29 over there,' pointing 'to see if it's possible for wheelchair access and things like that. I'm working for Brian.'

The woman removes her armour plate.

'Poor man,' she says. She walks back up the path and opens the door. 'Jodie, get out here!' she shouts.

It turns out her eldest, Jodie, has been out for a drink a few times with Brian.

'Jodie love, come out here,' she calls more softly.

A minute later a hard featured late twenties looking woman with her arms folded is standing right there. Jodie looks to have received all her family's allocation of intelligence.

'Did you know, sorry do you know Brian well?' I ask.

49

'Nah not really, we went out for a drink to that new bar round the corner once and a few times to the Park pub. Last time was this summer,' she smiles at remembering this. She laughs remembering something else,

'It was funny, right, we nearly got thrown out of the new bar because the barman gave Brian his drink in a jar. They all look weird in there like from Little House on the Prairie, braces and dungarees...'

'Amish?' I offer.

'Yeah, that's them, anyway so Brian started shouting at the barman, 'I WANT MY BEER IN A FUCKIN' JAM JAR I'LL ASK FOR IT. I WANT MINE IN A BOTTLE. YOU MENNONITE BASTARD!' I had to drag him away! I had to look up Mennonite on my phone when I got home,' she laughed.

'How long have you lived here?' I ask, beginning to take a shine to this seemingly perpetually laughing lass.

'All my life.'

'Why did your brother call it the soldier's house?'

'My brother,' she laughs, 'he's my son. We can't afford to get a place round here that's why we live with me ma.'

'Oh right.'

'Brian's always lived over there with his mum and dad. His dad died years ago but I remember him when I were growing up. He had an allotment my mum said, came home with veg now and again. He looked all grey and ghost-like mum said. He were a soldier, other folk round here said. I tell you what, that was one house we never trick or treated, tell you that for nowt. His mum were lovely and it were her who said it'd be nice if I took Brian out for a drink, y'know, just as friends. I think she knew she didn't have long to go and didn't want Brian to be left alone to fester.'

'I know this sounds a bit odd,' I start to say. In fact it's pretty unprofessional of me too but I can't seem to find the right moment to discover what happened to Brian. I look at Jodie and ask, 'it's not that I need to know this, it's not really my job but could you tell me what happened to him?'

'I heard he was attacked on a bus that's all. That's all I heard.'

We chat for another five minutes and I'm actually thinking of asking her myself if she wants to go for a drink as just friends but I don't think I'm ready for this. I'm not rebounding, I hit the floor and didn't bounce. I get in my car and wonder who could attack someone and leave that much mess. What was he attacked with? Something that popped his eye socket and peeled his head, scalped him!

The weather is still holding up and I park up easily and lug the bin liner up to my flat. Ten minutes later and I'm sat with a cup of coffee looking at Brian's diaries. I pick up a book at random and open it.

Peking IS the capital of China. Written like that, a big affirmative IS. I need to put the books in some semblance of chronological order so that I can start from the very beginning, a la Julie Andrews. I push the L-shaped sofa and small smoked-glass-topped circular coffee table to the side to give me a bit of floor space and start looking at the insides of the books for dates. The earliest books have some kind of wrapping paper on them, like wallpaper. I can't remember that ever being the done thing but hey-ho, each to their own. The first exercise book is dated 1990 when Brian was nine, full of spelling exercises and the like, drawings of Mummy and Daddy and Brian. There are five in all. After an hour I've gone through four of them and they're mainly school-related, ending in the mid-nineties. The fifth is different so I pop it to one side for a more thorough look.

I pick up the scrap album and notice the spine has come loose. Pages start to slide out that have real black and white photographs of Norman and Dorothy on their wedding day glued to them. Just the year, 1956 is written underneath the pictures. Other pictures on adjacent pages show more black and whites of Norman and others in uniform; smart shorn hair, eyes smiling, dates of 1949-55. There's an envelope from America which I open and see is from his brother with an address on it. I make a note to send a letter there. There are a handful of other letters from the Ministry of Defence which look interesting, mentioning in their titles The Korean War. Why did the little shit from across the street call it the soldier's house? Had it gained such standing in the area that it was a relevance? Not that I knew much about this conflict. I assumed that once World War Two was over it all went Cold, and then Vietnam happened. Was this country even fighting in The Korean War? If I had time I'd look into this. Getting bored now I flick past some old music magazine clippings and a local newspaper story from Christmas 1978.

Beans on toast with a poached egg and, *yay cheese again* is my stomach liner and in between eating and washing up the dishes I reálise that I'm not suited to surviving on a desert island, let alone one attached to the rest of humanity. Craving company I look window-wards and realise it's become Thursday night. Whilst I remember that I need at some point to download Brian's house schematic to my own laptop I realise my phone charge isn't sufficient for both this and a night out running the firework gauntlet. Night out wins.

I wake slightly hung-over, trying to picture what happened last night. Looking at the shrapnel on the bedside table I seem to have spent a few quid. I pick up a piece of scrap paper and, turning it, see what isn't my handwriting but a phone number and the name Amy; and I remember going off for food with a bunch of folk when the pub closed. Ended up at a new taco place round the corner called Buenos Nachos where I ended up having one of the pub staff telling me about the different types of keg beer I should be drinking, especially pumpkin at this time of year, and through which vessels. I zoned out and asked for a Moretti.

My girlfriend left, she said, because I'd become too staid and unwilling, unprepared and unable to embrace the future of technology, culture, diversity and choice. Hence I walked back to my flat, to my radio, my Netflix, my laptop and cassette playing car. She, and the guy who was presumably her new bloke, moved out with our Bose system, sound bar and an entire family of Alexa devices. *No imagination* she said. *Look at my CV that's as creative as anything,* I said. Maudlin and snorting back a tear I'd trudged up the steps to grab a cup of cocoa… for fucks sake.

FRIDAY 3rd November.

I slide gingerly out of bed as though I feel we're heading towards an end game of mattress chess, the springs taut on my thigh as I step out onto the floor. The mattress tries to reform to an approximation of its former self and instead makes an audible boing. I actually jump at the sound and the thought of the bed having some sort of AI. It takes a moment to work out what I need to do and in which order. First I check my phone charge. There's enough to download the schematic to my laptop and I start this process before grabbing a shower. Kettle boiled and tea poured I check the laptop. Once printed off at the office this will make a visually stunning end to my presentation.

The sun is trying, but looking out over the slate grey roofs Leeds looks as hard as it gets. Winter proper feels like it's on the way. Hangover marginally appeased I look at the laptop and see it's finished and is prompting me to open the jpeg. I tap on it and the house known as 29 Upper Park Crescent appears as if by magic. It shows a virtual house on a multi-dimensional axis that allows any CAD to totally redesign Brian's house – really impressive from one small app. I'll recommend to the team that it becomes standard operational software across our department for property modification. A further add-on would even work out material and construction costs. I'm practicing this spiel over and over; only all this is being said in silence because there's a hole under his house.

I stare at this for too long really. There is an explanation. I remember typing in the co-ordinates and gave four foot of under-floor which should come back as a thick black/dark grey line. Instead it's come up like something from the film Poltergeist; a house with all its ground-floor and upstairs in place but suspended over a gaping void.

Almost like a sinkhole. I'm now in no immediate hurry to

deliver this presentation and in fact need to do more background work on the client before the final presentation and recommendation, so I'll just return to complete this survey.

I message Mo and let her know that I'm finalising the structural part of my report and then I Google old images of Leeds; specifically Upper Park Crescent. Lo and behold, about 300 images in, up comes a picture from 1922 which clearly shows an uninterrupted row of sturdy Victorian terraced houses. The picture from 1965 shows the town houses instead. My immediate thought is a cellar cavity but my head spends minutes running through this… modern thirties town houses shouldn't have them. Turn of the century terraces do. My background knowledge of building tells me that you can't build a house on anything other than a solid base; whether hard-standing, foundations or footings to name but a few; unless it's a house boat or stilted and these aren't applicable in Headingley. Ok, that leaves the more likely scenario, to wit: Victorian terraces generally had large cellars; once the terrace is gone the cellar is filled with whatever's available, hardcore or something. On a solid base a new house is built. Therefore, I conclude this; there was a cellar, there wasn't a cellar, there is a cellar. I don't think I want to see the cellar. I want to see the cellar.

On the drive over, I'd pinned down where I think the cellar is and set myself this as a task, so upon opening the door, this time with torch, I'm standing in the pantry doorway in nine seconds. No wonder I hadn't seen this. I think my surprise at being confronted with 48 bottles of Kronenburg and some nuclear looking cider had made me overlook a small recessed handle in the lino-ed floor. Dragging the beer aside I look down and reach to grasp the semi circular handle. I give it a steady tug and this hatch, merely a lino covered wooden door shaped floor, opens and then rests flush against the back wall. Horror movie music is beginning to play in my mind but like a novice I'm going in.

The floor, lifted, reveals stone steps leading downwards: the original terraced house stairs. They lead down to a cellar. The builders must've stuck the houses on top of the old foundations. I wonder what might have caused the old terrace to come down – gas blast, German bombs. It doesn't mean anything but this procrastination only makes me want to go down there less than I did thirty seconds ago. Gingerly I start to edge my way down, feeling for a light switch along a rough wall, finding none, and then switching on the torch. Twelve steps down and I'm in a room that feels turn of the twentieth century. Surprisingly not damp, but cool and dark. My torch pans around picking up objects, shadows flitting up, a vice, a workbench, a filing cabinet and table, stone floor but with the odd off-cut of the same carpet as upstairs. A box with what looks like Meccano and Hornby models, model paints, a couple of test tubes on the table.

There is a faint but familiar smell and I see another hash-pipe and what appears to be a bong made out of a cider bottle. That isn't the familiar smell though and a small doorway in the cellar takes me through to another room, tapping the wall shows it to be just a stud wall. My beam takes in a metal shelf, then another, more. Floor to ceiling metal shelving all holding book after book after book. I move to one shelf and look at the titles. Craning my neck and the torch I start at the top. This is the smell I'd recognised, just like a second-hand book shop. The titles are another thing entirely and I realise that these are reference books, old too. I guess these were to be slung and Brian rescued them for his own private library. Marked with the Dewey Decimal system 200-and-something The Bible, The Koran, and Buddhism. 500 onwards, mechanical and engineering books mixed with medical text books, sports books, older than any of the books in the university I'd studied at.

I hear a creak upstairs and turn to go back up. I suddenly don't fancy being down here that much. As I bend down to go back through the door I get a crack on my head, a pain and a brief intense flash of light inside my skull.

'Fucking hell,'

I clutch my temple where I've been hit and sweep my torch round. Still in motion is a piece of wood swinging from the wooden door lintel in a cats' cradle of some sort. I'd missed it on the way in and now feel a lump coming up. In a useless theatrical manner I go down to the floor like I've been shot. I've seen videos of footballers over-exaggerate and I'm in danger of embarrassing myself, the only witness. So with my head hurting I see a low level solid camp bed, crawl to it and half sit, half lie down.

Shining the light at the ceiling I see that it's concrete and that it looks very solid. I see a light encased in a metal frame, almost military looking. From my side I spot the string pull for the light and tug it, it works and we have light. The room is painted with some sort of paint, probably distemper, just white. I make out a slight curvature in the ceiling, almost vaulted but not quite, strong though, and I think that with the floor boards and joists completely covering the footprint of the building, structurally it's fine. Nevertheless I am intrigued as to how this came about.

Is it relevant to the client and the case? *No, so move on*, Mo would say. Would it create more problems to notify someone of this? Probably. Can I ignore it? Ignore what?

'Atta boy,' I say.

I lay there for a good ten minutes rubbing my head and then spend the next half an hour going through this library. I find another orange exercise book and this one seems to be a current one. It's dated what, four months ago; it just says in really gouged-in writing,

Cardiff DO play at Ninian Park.

Ermm… I'm thinking no they don't.

I turn the page and it says,

CUNTS.

On the next page there are a couple of torn out pages from another book, an old football book stating that indeed Cardiff do play at Ninian Park and won the 1927 Cup Final. The other shows that Derby play at the Baseball Ground. I fold this notebook into my pocket and then spend another half hour playing with the Meccano set and other models.

The drugs paraphernalia explains a little of Brian's reluctance for me to see his house; the hidden cellar and more drugs explain a good bit more. What's his game? By the time I leave the house I've had another wander round, used the loo again and peered over the leaf mulched street.

I decide it's shopping time. Although it's Friday, it's a night I leave to the students now. I've been there before and don't fancy listening to some banging old school tune that's so new I don't remember it coming out in the first place. Instead I haul my bags for life up to the flat.

I'm finally, after weeks, starting to refill the cupboards after the break up left the house bereft as well as its tenant. I feel happy that the kitchen is bursting with food and cleaning products, the bathroom is full of stuff and my fridge is full of cheese, snacks and a craft artisanal beer as well as some normal beer that's brown and tastes of bitter. Anyway, I've got the craft one as an homage of sorts. Before turning my phone off I have a quick look and realise that I'm no longer the friend of my ex-girlfriend, but there is a friend request from Amy, go figure; I accept.

As the phone powers down I close the curtains, grab the beer and turn off the big light, crashing on the sofa and pressing play on the laptop.

I Blame Terrence Episode 2

Episode two starts in much the same vein as the first. The sign writer is crossing out the population of 13,989 and replacing it with 14,051. Another fifty-odd marketing experts have moved in. A series of people, sales managers, corporate sponsorship agents and executives door-stepping the Terrence household, long range telephoto lens shots of trainers being worn, socks, shirts, everything.

The soundtrack to this is more robo-folk, a bit Peter Bjorn and John meets Albarn's Gorillaz.

The trainers that Terrence wears aren't the leading brand and are really the best pair his mother could get him with her monthly clothing allowance. Nevertheless, her being a fastidious and caring all-American housewife means that Terrence is immaculately turned out in his Airframe trainers and they look pretty cool. Within a week they're America's number one selling trainer. Terrence is shown sitting having some granola or some other cereal when his father comes home with a cheque in his hand hollering

'Terrence my boy, YOU are our ticket outta here!'

I take a sip of my salted caramel lychee gose and wordlessly put it down.

Throughout the next twenty or so minutes of this episode Terrence is subjected to every humiliation going. It's actually very funny as his underpants are taken from the washing line and a hasty ad campaign tells the nation:

Hey Terrence wears them - why don't you!?

It's funny but actually from a practical point it's not so crazy a concept. I feel some sympathy here for Terrence because his mother's bought the best clothes value for money wise that she can.

Terrence gets a migraine and his diligent mother takes him to the local health centre. Two days later the health care centre floats publicly for millions of dollars pushing the idea *Terrence comes to us, you should too.* It's funny but risky for the boy, as the uneasiness is creeping in that some firms may want to stop

Terrence because he isn't endorsing their products. Poor Terrence isn't endorsing anyone, he's piggy in the middle. The camera focuses on the stash of cheques between his dad's sausage-sized fingers. The first episode showed his dad's fingers to be much thinner. I guess next week his fingers will be the size of a baseball mitt, a banana hand. The big businesses that are missing out are starting to stir and the executive boardrooms are shown in the episode with massive blood splashes pulsing over the walls like a slasher movie. The fact that everyone wants a USP and the dad wants a meal ticket is the unfortunate side effect. Terrence, being right in the middle is beginning to stir.

The show finishes with the cereal that Terrence was eating being bulk processed into millions of boxes and, having been fork-lifted onto huge rigs, sent all over the States. Terrence is back by his tree, sweating and rocking gently back and forth. The show finishes with a brown envelope being passed to a shady looking character, possibly a hit-man. I don't put on episode three as I want to eke it out. It's funny enough now but I feel it's going bubble up soon to be a cracker.

I shut down the lap top and get up wearily. I pour the salted caramel lychee gose down the sink and go to bed thinking of the cellar defences at Brian's.

SATURDAY 4ᵗʰ November.

The weekend is upon me and this is a time when I feel particularly listless. The weather is nice enough not to have to spend the day wrapped up in bed so I get up. I'm halfway through my coffee when I remember the party I've been invited to tonight. That settles me down somewhat and I get dressed with a purpose. I hop on a bus, it's strangely easier to get around at the weekend without using a car, and head to the big library. It's a big and bold Victorian building with a dozen steps to its front revolving door. I push on through and actually ask to become a member, which a driving licence and utility bill allows me to be. Five minutes later I'm looking at the thirteen books it has shelved on the Korean War. I pull out the potted version, a bit Horrible Histories if you like but it sums it up. I actually don't even know why I'm here at all. This is me pushing my sad weekend life into the margins so to speak.

The Korean War 25 June 1950 to 27 July 1953

The first page tells me that sixteen countries made up the UN response to a protracted wrangle over unification after WWII by North Korea. A swift invasion into the South followed with the help of China and Russia. Welcome to the Korean War which leads to the smash hit TV series MASH, a movie of the same name and a number one hit record about suicide: 100,000 from Britain, and just short of 4,502 servicemen never to be the same again. 1,078 dead, over 2,500 wounded, and 1,000-odd prisoners of war or missing in action. National Service was extended by six months and a number of these young National servicemen came home to Victoria Crosses.

One battle, it says, had 600 servicemen pitched against 30,000

Chinese. Quotes from soldiers said it was like the Blitzkrieg one minute and medieval warfare the next, nothing like the envisioned first jet-age war. Freezing winter and living in cold wet trenches. Most notably about 10% of the POWs were re-educated by the enemy.

I don't like the sound of our soldiers being re-educated by our Cold War enemies, it makes *me* cold thinking about it.

At the war's end the enemy spent so long repatriating the prisoners that some of the brainwashed prisoners just stayed.

This I find largely inconceivable and struggle to even think about indoctrination, although most of my course modules looked specifically into grooming and child sexual exploitation, and all the case studies I'd read were on historic abductions and Stockholm syndrome. *All the terrible things people do and the even worse things that parents will do. Parasites.* None of this is going to help me with my presentation for Brian's recovery plan and I close the book and pop it back on the shelf. I shuffle out of the library and find a bottle shop in the big arcade.

Back in my flat, I unload the three artisan beers that cost me more than I wanted to pay and then the normal shopping, including a four pack of normal brown beer. I put all this and the other food away and slump onto the sofa with my mobile. I while away two hours swapping between my survival game and Cubescape, still on level 1,300. Survive has me at level 99 and I'm fashioning a motorboat but unless I spend real money I'm stuck because I'm certain that the petrol tank doesn't exist in the normal game. The fireworks have started early in my flat today.

SUNDAY 5th November.

I'm awake early having no hangover but then remembering I only had my cans and not the three bottles. The party last night was fine and I got on better than I thought with my neighbours, who I think were showing a degree of sympathy for my relationship status and were probably relieved to no longer have to listen to me being shouted at for being boring. Mentally I tell myself to stop being boring and actually laugh out loud. I get up and dress. The fridge boasts new milk and I pop the kettle on, wandering over to the window to see that nothing is stirring on the street. I look down to the pile of letters and read the oldest one. It's a letter from the Ministry of Defence responding, it seems, to a Mrs. Ball's request to the whereabouts of Norman. The kettle clicks and I make instant coffee, half a sugar, milk, same old. I'm bugged though because Norman didn't marry Dorothy until 1956. I grab a piece of scrap paper and write down the dates, thinking that I hope Brian appreciates how much effort I'm putting into this conundrum about his dad. Fact is, I very much like doing the Einstein style puzzles. The lines of positive and negative information that you tick off on a grid until you find that Tom is Italian, eats pineapple, plays soccer and drives a Zeppelin. Rose is German drinks milkshake but doesn't play the fiddle. The one who drives the ambulance doesn't have a lion.

Ten minutes later and I'm re-reading the letter to confirm, as it had said all along: *We will of course notify you as soon as we hear any news of your son Norman… etc. etc. MOD.* This is dated December 1950. Looking at the figures again I sit down. It seems Norman fell into National Service age by about a month. Christ, one month later and he'd have missed it. Somehow a year and a half in and he ended up in Korea. Again, another few months and he'd have probably avoided it altogether by completing his service. Was this an error that ended up with Norman in a war? Worse, he was missing in action. Talk about unlucky. My mind is blown by this and I decide, as early as it is, I'm going to head up to the cafes on the main drag to get a coffee and a Sunday paper. The drizzle is more than just a drizzle and I realise it's bonfire night finally. Not much is happening on the main road other than that the two neighbouring cafes are open. The first telling the neighbours that it's the first plant based vegan restaurant in the area and the second saying it was the first artisanal vegetarian bistro in the city. Either of them want to charge me an hour's wage for a deconstructed flat white with almond milk and a pistachio flapjack. I keep walking and find a coffee and a full English in a café where I read the paper for an hour.

On my amble back to the flat I bump into Amy walking along the path between the ridge and the main road. I recognise her from when we'd all ended up in the new taco place and realise she's a barmaid from the pub. I say hello and ask why she's up so early; she's working later. She said that it wasn't a come on, the other night giving me her phone number but that she was interested in what I'd been saying. To be honest, I can't really remember what that was. She reminds me that the course she's on part-time is media based and that the main thrust of her studies at the moment is the rise of the micro-influencers. She says I'd scoffed at this, and she wanted to actually write down my views on the subject for a project she was doing. We don't arrange anything but I say I'll message her and we can do this thing over some weird beer for her and something approaching normal for me. She laughs and I have a spring in my step all the way back to the flat.

When I get back I download the MASH theme by Johnny Mandel and as depressing as it is it's ten times better than some of the dross on my tapes. I flick through Brian's two *interesting* books.

THE THUMB PUSH BASE OF THE DRAWING PIN IS TOO THICK AND NEEDS TO BE APPROXIMATELY HALF THIS. THE PIN ITSELF NEEDS TO BE ABOUT A TENTH OF ITS LENGTH. THE PAINT NEEDS TO BE A MATCH FOR THE THUMB LATCH. A TENTH OF ITS LENGTH AND A MATCH FOR THE LATCH.

A little diagram shows what appears to be a door handle, the thumb press type. On it is a filed down drawing pin. A bit horrified by this I see that the aim of this game is to have someone press down on the latch and break skin, prick the finger and I can imagine the unlucky recipient immediately placing the injured appendage in their mouth and sucking. Nice, I don't think.

DAD'S SHED DOOR, NEED ADHESIVE, PAINT.

In the other notebook more:

IT'S NOT TSB BANK IT'S JUST TSB.

IT'S NOT PIN NUMBER IT'S JUST PIN.

Then more:

USING THE SMALLEST DRILL BIT AND TAPE I'VE MANAGED TO MAKE A HOLE IN THE MUG WITH THE HANDLE ON THE RIGHT. THE HOLE IS THE SIZE OF A PENCIL. HAVE CHIPPED AWAY AT SOME OF THE GLAZE AND THEN USED THE MIXTURE OF SUGAR AND ICING SUGAR TO FILL IN THE HOLE. SMOOTHED IT DOWN UNTIL IT SET AND WAS HARD. I PUT IT BACK IN THE CUPBOARD. DAD IS AT THE ALLOTMENT.

Then more:

LIFT OUT THE ENTIRE CEREAL BAG AND TURN IT OVER CAREFULLY. SEPARATE THE SEALED JOINT IN THE BAG AND PLACE THE BOX BACK OVER IT UPSIDE DOWN. TURN AND PLACE BACK ON THE SHELF.

FISHING LINE ATTACHED TO THE PORCH OVERHANG WITH A SMALL STONE AND A LONGER PIECE OF LINE ALLOWS YOU TO REMOTELY KNOCK ON THEIR DOOR; THERE IS NEVER ANYONE THERE.

The notes are a mixture of what seem like petty annoyances made into angry reactions and practical, no, nasty jokes; although the effort required seems to be disproportionate to the pay-off. I mean, how long would it take to drill a hole in a mug without it shattering and then re-glaze it with a substance that would dissolve and cover the drinker in maybe a couple of mils of tea down their shirt? The upshot would be to see that the cup had cracked and throw it in the bin and get another.

Who picks up the actual cereal packet anyway? Surely you'd just pick up the box? And even if you did pick up the packet you'd only disgorge the cereal from that. You'd achieve what? A box full of cereal, now deteriorating.

Ghost tapping a neighbour's door, like why?

My mind is drifting; admittedly to thoughts of the difficult level 1,300 of Cubescapes and I put the book down and pick up my phone.

MONDAY 6th November.

Case numbers two and three fall into my lap. They seem straightforward but don't they all? Eighty year old has fallen outside her house and is currently in hospital. What modifications are we going to put in place in order for her to live a normal life back at home?

Next a referral to see if we can build a partition wall in one of our rental's bedrooms, so that the five children are segregated into their respective sexes. This is all delivered by Mo in a meeting, scheduled last week that I'd not picked up on. It seems that the powers that be are reasonably satisfied with the speed (slow), of the pilot and want to measure our capacity. Somebody questions whether we're being given too much work as the job is becoming bigger than day sized or more than one person can do in a day, or case. I've now got three cases, which will spread out my client-centred stuff. The questioner is fed the office mantra, *brave new country, Dunkirk spirit, Blitz mentality*; nobody in charge and headless chickens spring to mind. I stare at Mo and almost feel like putting my hand up to speak. The other case workers shuffle their new tasks and I sit until it's just Mo and me in the room.

'Mo,' and she stops me with a hand held up like a traffic cop on duty.

'Yes, you've maybe noticed that all the property modifications that have come in are now in your possession,' she says 'it's just expedient at the moment.'

'That wasn't it, Mo,' I say, but it wasn't something I'd noticed either 'my feeling Mo is this, who signs this stuff off?'

'You do,' she says, 'what's the matter, don't you feel qualified enough?'

'Err... frankly no,' I say 'I'm not time served.'

'What?!' she says 'do you think that the lifers out there who've spent thirty years doing this job are more qualified than you? This is the now and the future. I don't need someone slapping me down with "issues". I don't need someone spoon feeding the world. I need to know where the router will go. Where the Wi-Fi hot spots are. Would a serving hatch work? Would a home tutor help? I need to future-proof lives, not mollycoddle and fuck 'em up, give out sweets and platitudes. Think outside of the...'

'Box,' I finish.

Mo smiles.

'I had a memo today saying that there was an over-reliance on, get this - *Big Kit* energy. What do you suppose that is? And that instead of thinking turn up the gas, I've now to consider putting windmills and solar panels in these adapted builds. I'm not a social worker I'm turning into an office wonk.'

She's flagging, but goes gamely on.

'We're the brutal face of sort-it-out Britain. The country is tired of being victim-driven, so they tell me. We want this brave entrepreneurial problem-solving, eco-friendly, planet saving, world leading iron fist in a velvet glove.'

Mo's face has reddened considerably and she sits down.

'Glass of water boss?' I ask.

'Glass of fucking gin,' she replies.

'Do I get to see these new cases, the people I mean?'

'Do you need to?' replies Mo.

'I don't know who decides, is it a conveyor belt now?' I say.

I'm trying to get a picture of what the management want but it seems to alter minute by minute, not case by case; knee jerk reactions to external pressure.

'Just call it stress-testing our protocols and systems to see if we can operate as a unilateral agency.'

'Do what?' I say.

'Well, rather than involve other departments at this stage, see if we can order building redesigns or medical interventions,' Mo calmly says but with no conviction.

She could clearly see my unease and spent the next half an hour bolstering my confidence.

'You were entertaining guests in a chalet, cooking, sorting out menus with the chef. How hard would you find it to put together an economical and varied food plan for anyone?'

'So I'm thinking would Brian like his fondue on a Monday and his croque-monsieur and spanakopita later in the week,' I say. Mo angrily tells me to shut up.

'You worked in property. Look Simon, these are transferable skills that put together should make you a good worker and prospect for future progression in this sector.'

I leave the office and try to remember what Gav the chalet chef had once said, something along the lines of pressure being temporary but stress being permanent. I feel that Mo is, if not already there, imminently arriving at permanently stressed. I need to give my head a wobble.

I sit at my hot-desk, thinking. I know fuck all about helping this man. I've no external help and the only thing I do know is so contradicted by other people's testimony. Almost a Jekyll and Hyde. He's quiet, he ain't. He's calm, yeah, as fuck. The only common denominator is... *think, think, think.* I get my mobile out. I contact the Parks and Recreation department which is I guess about eight doors away from the office and ask about allotment owners' details.

At first they tell me not politely to mind my own business citing Data Protection. After I wield Mo as the nuclear option she's told to do one as well. The Director is brought into the fight and he speaks to their Service Director. The threat level is creeping up with every call. To stop this escalating to the Under Secretaries of State for Housing, Health, Data Security and the Home Office, the Director calls me and Mo into his office where he asks if I actually need this info. I'm part of the way between cross, nervous and uselessly sad. I tell them that yes, Brian's dad died years ago but that throughout all of this investi… sorry, case, everyone has mentioned his allotment and I merely want to know if it's still his. Will it need modifying? Could we sell it? I'm clutching at straws.

'All this for that!?' shouts the Director, 'fuck-a-nory, I'll have to have more than that!' He loudly shuts the door and I'm left sitting with Mo.

'Are you alright?' she asks.

'Yeah, I'm fine,' I reply 'I've been doing this case for less than a week, Mo and already I'm getting my presentation sorted. I got Geraldine to send a letter to Brian's brother through an old address I found in his stuff.'

Mo gurns, bottom lip out, nearly touching the bottom of her nose, and I'm reminded by her that we don't have any of his stuff.

'His house plans are nearly ready and I've submitted a request for Geraldine to ask if the insurance company want to push this through more quickly using my file notes. I'm doing okay.'

'How quickly can you move on from this case?' Mo asks.

'What do you mean?'

'Have you been given a date when we can move this case onto, say, our Care Resource team?'

'Not yet, Mo,' I say, 'it'll be the New Year before they'll even consider him medically fit to leave the care home and he won't even leave then if the house isn't ready.'

Mo is thinking. I can see her eye twitch and she's looking to my right, not through me but not seeing me either.

'Is this one going to be our responsibility anyway?' Mo randomly throws out. 'I hear the words insurance settlement, redundancy payout, inheritance, I mean this thing has virtually no prospect of passing any means-test anytime soon, am I right?'

'Clinical, a bit harsh Mo, but probably true,' I reply.

'Don't get too stuck on it,' she says and right then the door opens and the Director has a large sheaf of papers in his hand. He hands them to me and says tersely,

'I've had to stick my neck out for sight of these. We don't have power over a unitary authority so if this gets any publicity it will be called a snoopers charter and we'll all be up the creek without a paddle. As it is I've err... borrowed these for, err have you a paper shredder at home?'

'Yes,' I lie.

'You know what GDPR is?'

'Yes.' Not a lie.

'Get these out of the office, I never saw them, get what you need and destroy. Understand?'

'Yes.'

I leave his office and can hear him telling Mo that we need some good news, some early results and that he wished the architect of the pilot had done a real job, a proper job on it. Funny, because it's *his* baby. Mo's voice is getting louder and she's starting to have a real go. I hear him also raise his voice and say he's not going to throw her under the bus. I wince at this and set off through the office for home.

That whole shambles has taken up the afternoon and I've missed lunch so head off to the parade near my flat for an early tea.

Not quite understanding or knowing how, I'm standing in the vegan place. I look at the glass front counter and try to make out the food stuffs in there. The thing I'm staring at looks a little like a dog turd.

'It's like dolmas,' the woman behind the counter says 'except we use birch or oak instead of vine leaves; it's a bit more of a rugged flavour this time of year as there's quite a high tannin concentration so we steep them overnight. Then we re-purpose the water for our chicory and acorn coffee. The garnish is dandelion, we grow them in the cellar. Obviously we won't grow them in autumn so we harvest them around April or May and freeze-pack them. The French force them like rhubarb,' she says to nobody. 'The flowers in the park over the road we don't use, well, because we don't know their provenance.'

Yes you fucking do! I want to scream.

'They're also quite bitter, so we use the early shoots. We use them in our other cooking too, but due to their bitterness we change the water a couple of times. Don't worry though because that becomes the infusion that we use for the older shoots. We roast them and with the water, that's your coffee substitute. Would you like a cup, it's one of the super foods?' she says. 'It's a diuretic and a laxative as well so it's a great cleanser internally.'

What a bloody boring monologue. I look at this robotic waitress and ask if she can do a normal cup of tea. She literally sneers before going to the kettle and then slamming a cupboard door that was open before opening another and slamming that too before appearing with a tea bag.

'Do you want anything with this?'

'What, like almond milk and pomegranate sugar?' I ask. She perks up briefly until I say "naww, just normal full fat if you've got it.'

'No,' she says firmly. 'This is a vegan restaurant. Soya, almond, hazelnut or pea milk?'

'Black.'

In the end I go to the kebab shop for their take on chicken and chips which I eat in my flat, as deflated as I could be. My reading material tonight will be a catalogue of names of people who have had or indeed still have an allotment. Eligibility and charisma: none.

Looking at the city's allotment records I find the north-west section. There are loads. I make a cup of tea and sift through the stack. The top sheet gives an overview of the information, together with general plot details. There's a waiting list although nobody knows how long you will wait. It unwraps this by saying once your tenancy agreement is approved and your small annual rent is received it's yours for as long as you want; looks like a sixty foot by twenty foot plot can be yours for about thirty quid, half size plots for those that don't need that much veg are also available. The only criteria are that you keep it in good shape and order and don't use any of your amenities, I guess shed, for any illegal activity or use that may contradict the local byelaws of the borough. *Fuck me when was this written?* They aren't in alphabetical order but plot number and there's a plan of the site with each plot numbered and their relation to each other. It looks like a poor attempt to recreate the Père Lachaise cemetery map, but here the plots are occupied by Smiths, Smeatons and Browns rather than Piafs, Wildes and Chopins. Halfway through my tea, milk and one sugar, I find the plot. Plot 94 (half-size) was acquired by a Mrs. Dorothy Agnes Ball in June 1960.

The allotment was relinquished, I believe, on the final settlement of Dorothy's probate, in that the solicitor or executor had passed a copy of her death certificate to the Parks and Allotments department. It looks like it was inventoried and a number of tools were returned to Brian. The process of exchange from one party to another could take up to twenty six weeks although three months was the likely timeframe for transference of a plot. Anyway, plot 94 was now in the hands of a redacted name. There, just crossed out.

Clicking on the laptop and finding the file I start up Terrence.

I Blame Terrence Episode 3

The opening credits appear. A Cine film all scratchy shows a small kid with Buddy Holly glasses being chased by, one can only assume, bullies; running across a grassed yard with a water sprinkler spraying a creosote-painted fence. Clearly trying to depict I guess, small town America, and then the music starts, some weird robo-folk tune with the spliced axing riff from Radiohead. The credits continue with a fast forward through junior school, the boy is still running, being chased through to prep school, high school and coffee shops then white picket fences before juddering to a halt and the Cine reel rewinding back to the coffee shop. At this point three words appear as if branded onto the screen:

I Hate Terrence.

The Hate word is then erased and the word Blame replaces it.

A town sign says Anniesburg, OR, Pop 14,100.

Terrence decides. He goes to the local mall in darkness, you see him dodging from street lamp to street lamp. It's a long walk and we pick him up just as the mall opens and the delivery trucks are fuelling up the concessions with their comestibles for the day or depositing other more durable stock. Terrence gingerly wanders the mall's shops, whilst muzak plays in the background, until he finds what he's looking for. The scene cuts to his house where his mother knocks on his bedroom door and gently asks,

'Terrence?' walking in to find the room empty. A note is on his newly made bed, it just says *Gone Shopping.*

The next scene shows Terrence in and out of dressing rooms looking in mirrors; either approving with a nod or giving a disapproving tut and going back to the changing room. Next it's the shoe shop and... well, the clock hands spin round. See, this is where it's formulaic. It's doing all the generic things you'd expect from an American based sit-com, but you do feel for Terrence.

This then cuts away to show a car parked near Terrence's house. It's early morning, certainly too early for the marketing types to be door-stepping the house. The driver slides a photograph from the brown envelope of the previous episode across. Sure enough it's a 7 x 5 of Terrence dressed in the country's best selling trainers plus his beige flannel trousers and white granddad shirt. Two hours pass, then another half hour and the boy turns the door handle and looks at his startled parents.

'Terrence what on Earth have you got on?'

'I went shopping.'

'Is that a wig?'

'No, Dad.'

'Terrence, go to your room! That's an order.'

There's a knock on the door and Terrence's mum answers it to a man with a clipboard. Behind him is a small truck with the name of the shop in the mall that Terrence was last at, emblazoned on the side.

'Ma'am, please sign for these, it's free from all of us at Jansson Haberdasher & Hardware for the great endorsement that Terrence gave us today.'

He turns and next we see him wheeling a pallet of goods into the family garage. The goods range from a sewing machine and badge making equipment through a coffee machine to a button stamp, cobblers' last and various bales of material: denim, flannel, leather. The man in the car with the 7 x 5 photograph hasn't recognised the new look Terrence and starts his car to report the lack of news to his paymasters.

Terrence is in the last scene with sheets of tattoos. They aren't real, they're the ones you place on your arm and press down on with warm water. The time warp thing happens again and we see that in the last two hours Terrence has virtually covered his body in tats. Mermaids and anchors, a moustache, anvils and geometric circles, motorbikes, pirates, couple of butterflies, feathers, a leopard head being half man and half cat. Missed out on the swallows, barbed wire and scissor cuts that wouldn't have looked out of place in this country I think. The end credits start to roll and Queens.of the Stone Age play. The last thing we see is a label on a big cardboard box that says Icelandic Volcanic Pumice.

TUESDAY 7th November.

We have a winner in our office today! Rachel's managed to get one of her clients a damp proof course installed in their ground-floor flat at the tax-payers' expense rather than the private landlord's. Her client has a persistent bad chest and her three year and one year old children will also have this problem unless we rectify the cause - rising damp. This dream scenario floats around our unit and yet somehow the idiocy of this is completely lost on the

Director. The client is on benefits and we've paid the contractor so when she gets pregnant again she'll demand that *we,* the council, re-house her due to lack of space and the fact that the private landlord has put the rent up for his newly damp free flat. Notwithstanding that anyone who knows buildings would make sure that the basement flat was tanked properly, thus rendering this fix unnecessary. In anyone's book I'd call that a shocking result but on 'Planet CRASH' it's our biggest win. Honestly, you couldn't make it up. The Director's organised for the local paper to come to the office and in front of all of us is saying,

'All of our staff are located, ermm… live, around the areas that they work; we call it, not Care in the Community but more Core of the Community. We are the strength!'

Someone behind me whispers *'for fucks sake'* and coughs loudly. On the way out of the press briefing we're collectively shaking our heads at spin being put on what is basically a fortunate working pattern. I could be working across the city next week. We file out back to our hot-desks or whatever we can find to work on.

The rest of today and all of the next is taken up in dealing with the two cases that had dropped into my lap. The eighty year old would come out of hospital to see that a new handrail had been installed from gate to door and the bedroom partition had been authorised by me to be completed ASAP by our own rental service team. At no point was I used in assessing whether there were any other underlying issues that could have resulted in these scenarios. Pass the parcel. These jobs were organised in something like two four-minute phone calls and the remaining time was filling out paperwork. A day and a half, all paperwork and I was already firing most of it at Geraldine. I think that most of the office if not all of us are chucking paperwork at Geraldine.

This week I've decided I'll try out some of the other eateries and places on the parade so I park and wheel lock my car and walk the short trip up the road. The occasional gun shot is heard... in reality it's a random firework left over from last week, but could still be a gun shot.

The make up of this parade goes, from right to left: corner shop, pub, estate agent, vegan restaurant, artisanal bistro, bottle bar, estate agent, kebab shop, tapas bar, bistro, Turkish barber, fancy dress shop. There's a 'To Let' sign over the tapas bar and a flyer in the window saying that 'Melody Leeds' is coming. It says on the flyer that a beer shop selling second-hand vinyl is opening. *Whatever fucking next?* I smirk.

I'm in the bottle shop which is a bit of a misnomer as it has two beer pumps on the counter. It's not small or large and has a floor-to-ceiling glass front. This window is broken up by a shelf pretending to be a breakfast bar, that I'm now settled on a stool at, looking out onto the road. There's a paper rack that has a local and a national in it but I pick out the local. I flick a beer mat onto the breakfast bar and go to the counter to get a drink.

To say I'm miffed is something of an understatement but there's nothing I can do. I'd been to the counter, newspaper under my arm and looked at the menu, which was a sheet of paper on the back wall. I couldn't really read it all that clearly and there were a couple of students sat at a table watching me. It felt like they were waiting for me to make a mistake or something.

'Hi err... just one of them,' I said, pointing to a tap on the counter.

'The NEIPA?' asked the man behind the bar; he had a twisted beard like it'd been plaited.

'Yeah pint of that then.'

He was already pouring it and handed it to me saying,

'Just schooners or halves in here, buddy.'

I'd just handed over a tenner and pocketed the change.

So, in the five minutes I've been sitting here I've counted how many bottles are on sale as opposed to cans and actually the cans outnumber the bottles sixty-forty. The rain-stained pavement reflects headlights and it feels heavy, dense, the buses moving glacially through the lights at the junction. I'm drinking a schooner whatever the fuck that is. I feel slightly embarrassed; I'd dodged some ridicule because I'd tried to act nonchalant but now I'm stuck with something that looks like a pint but isn't. I shudder to think what it cost. I casually look it up on my phone. I spell it like the ship because I'm guessing, and see it's two thirds of a pint and there on the glass is the line saying two thirds. Then I check that NEIPA is New England India Pale Ale. Mine isn't pale it looks... I can't see through it; I thought I'd be looking through it. I take a sip. I stop myself right there and have a quiet word.

'Be less boring and a bit more Zen.'

Unfolding the paper, my eyes drift across some of the

adverts and then stare into space and I think of the Einstein puzzles. *The person who drinks the half-pint has paid £4. The can drinker is the Hipster. The person who paid £4 doesn't drink stout. The bitter drinker is not you. The stout drinker is not vegan. The person drinking pumpkin drinks from a can. The person who pays £4 drinks bitter. The pumpkin beer is not £4. The person who pays £5 is the Hipster.*

I take another drink and think it tastes like fruit juice, mango or something. The beer we drank at the chalet was just supermarket French bottled bier. My own student bar just had the stuff that paid the Student Union the most in sponsorship. I guess I missed the boat on this new style beer. *The person who drinks stout doesn't drink from a bottle. The half-pint drinker drinks bitter. The bottle is not pumpkin beer. Brian Bottle is definitely not drinking pumpkin beer.*

The traffic outside is grimly making its way home and the temperature is dropping like a stone as the door opens and some young students pour in.

The Hipster doesn't pay £6. The person who pays £6 is not vegan. The person who drinks IPA pays £3. The person who drinks bitter is the student. The person who drinks stout is not the Hipster.

The local rag leads with the library service wanting volunteers. Midway through the paper, I can only think I'd call it crims week, are reports of burglaries, drug driving, twoccing and the occasional pub assault. Property week at the back and that's the paper done.

I can't say how much I paid other than I've worked out it

would be £9 a pint. I finish my fruit juice schooner, do up my coat and walk the five minutes to my flat.

WEDNESDAY night 8th November.

I make it to the Frame and Painter, a typical big chain pub, high ceilings, menus from dawn to dusk, and see the three of them sharing a bottle of wine: buy two large glasses and the rest of the bottle is free. I understand the workings out here; for not too much outlay they each get a bottle's worth. Trying not to be too conspicuous I walk past them before turning to the ever-glamorous Miss Reid and say my hellos. I've got a beer in my hand and see a sign on the wall for Quiz Night with a gallon of beer to the winner. I ask them if they do the quiz and Helen says yes, just for a giggle, though at this one of the others says,

'Do you remember that week when Brian was with us and that round was on football grounds?'

'Do I?!' says the other giggling.

'What happened?' I ask.

'Well, Brian answered all ten. I mean, we don't do sport but Brian was really confident.'

'And?'

'Well, he got one right, couldn't tell you which one but he went bright red and …'

'You had to calm him down didn't you, Helen? Wait, it was Elland Road that was the only one he got right. I thought he was going to lose the plot there. It was quite unexpected,' she finishes.

All I can think of is the outburst in his book, swearing that Cardiff played at a ground they'd not played at for what… ten years? Why would he have said Ninian Park?

They ask me if I want to stay for the quiz but I say no. It feels like it was more some private lush club than a support group. These saved workers and Brian, who I can only feel sorry for. I still wouldn't have put his shoes on or climbed into his head but I want to help him more. I leave the Frame and Painter and catch the bus back home. I hop off on the main road and decide to have a beer in the, give them the benefit of the doubt, bottle shop.

In the bottle shop I see the hand-written tombstone sign offering an almost out of date micro-keg of something called Beetle Geuse at 6.42% ABV for a fiver. That sounds like a good deal; like the party sized beers in the supermarket. So I ask for one and hand over my fiver. The bartender, I realise I shouldn't call him that as he's only a shop assistant, turns around and gives me an empty half glass and pops next to it, a can. When I clearly start to rile at this he says,

'Technically it's a can but as we put on the sign that it's 330ml we can call it a nano or micro keg,' and then finishes off with,

'Pal.'

I take it and sit in the window. A couple of young students sitting around an up-ended wooden barrel for a table, are eyeing me up like I'm the enemy, or a dinosaur. The can states it was made

85

using cochineal. I look across to the shop assistant and ask what the Geuse is and he says,

'It's named that because of its style, a Gueuze because it's a sour beer made from two brews; don't mistake it for a Gose. It's called Geuse because of its strength 6.42, and also as in the star Betelgeuse is 642.5 light years away and Beetle because it's got, well… beetle juice in it.'

The beer is indeed sour. I feel forced to drink it as it cost a fiver. Thrifty, a trait I like to think I share with Yorkshire people. I finish it and leave the can and glass on the side but go up to the bar.

'Cochineal isn't a beetle,' I say 'it's a bug.'

'Well a ladybug's a beetle,' the shop assistant retorts 'and anyway who gives a fuck?' laughing with his two henchmen.

I can only answer back with,

'You shouldn't even call yourself a bottle shop either. You've more cans than bottles!' I mentally tell myself not to come here again.

He calls me mental and says maybe it's best if I don't come here again.

Back home whilst waiting for the kettle to boil for my night's tea I pick up some loose letters from Brian's stack of paper and come across a letter from the Central Library dated July asking Brian to come along to an appointment to discuss where there might be some positive movement forward following the decision to make him redundant. *Great news*, I smile. Anyway, underneath this,

attached by a paper clip, is another letter. A letter from Brian…
except it isn't. It's a draft and so is the page beneath, page two. I
guess he'd written and sent the final finished result except these two
pages; hand-written:

DEAR SIR, I WAS TRAVELLING ON THE NUMBER 41 AT
12.50 ~~ON TUESDA~~ TODAY ~~WHEN THE DRIVER.~~ I DON'T GO
ON BUSES OFTEN AND I ASKED THE DRIVER WHERE I
NEEDED TO GET OFF. HE TOLD ME HE'D SAY BUT HE
DIDN'T. SHIT. HE LAUGHED AT THE LAST MOMENT AND
SAID I'D MISSED IT. I GOT UP AND CAUGHT MY JACKET
ARM ON SOMETHING AND AT THIS POINT THE DRIVER
SLAMMED THE BRAKES ON. I WAS PITCHED FORWARD
AND NEARLY FELL. ~~I TORE MY JACKET~~; THE ARM OF MY
JACKET WAS NEARLY RIPPED RIGHT OFF. WHEN I
STARTED TO COMPLAIN THE DRIVER SAID THAT THE
POLICY WAS FOR THE COMPANY TO PAY FOR ANY
DAMAGE AND THAT I HAD TO GET OFF THE BUS, HE
LOOKED ME IN THE EYE AND SAID HE'D THROW ME OFF IF
I DIDN'T FUCK OFF. HE TOLD ME TO GET THE FUCK OFF
HIS BUS. I HAD AN APPOINTMENT THAT I COULDN'T KEEP
AND I'M SO FUCKING MAD.

Page two is the same letter with less swearing but more
anger:

I DON'T KNOW HIS NAME BUT I'VE SEEN HIM. I'D
RECOGNISE THAT SHIT.

I wonder if Brian managed to temper both the anger and
swearing for the final letter. The page is so deeply gouged that
Brian, well, he could have been writing this with a knife it was that
deep. I'm cross just reading it and wonder what the reply had said.

Actually, on a third sheet there's the start of a *Dear* but under this it just says,

WHAT'S THE BASTARD POINT?

It feels to me like he was up against it, fighting a battle he couldn't win. I'm even beginning to question whether he'd actually sent a letter or whether he was just venting his spleen. There isn't an address or a department on the drafts. *How frustrating,* I think. After my recent experience at the bottle shop I can only sympathise with him and I take myself off to the dent. I dream about Brian and me fighting a large stag beetle down a road with ladybirds cheering us on.

THURSDAY 9th November.

We'd speculatively written to America after the letter cropped up with Brian's brother's name and address on it. It was a letter thanking his mum for the picture of a young Brian in his first school uniform, the same school it says that Donald went to, hoping that Dad's alright, that was the gist of it. It was dated sometime in the mid-eighties and I wasn't holding out a lot of hope. I'd borrowed the office Dictaphone and after having been shown what to do because it was that ancient, instructed Geraldine to tell Brian's brother that I'd been assigned to Brian to help him convalesce. I didn't go into detail about Brian's injuries because it wouldn't achieve much and anyway, I wanted to get a picture of Brian: childhood, friends, that sort of thing.

So it's a bit of a happy shock when I receive an email. I'd

given out my own email address, but didn't expect such a quick response. Like, under a week later.

Hi Simon,

First of all thank you for notifying me of Brian's accident. I've never seen Brian in the flesh. I have a couple of photographs of him that I was sent and vice versa. I doubt that he would have much of an idea about me. If I could help you in any way I would, but the thing is I live in the States with my wife and daughter and to be frank the last place I'd be right now is in England.

I left England when I was in my early twenties and settled in America and about thirty years ago in California. My childhood and upbringing in England in the 60's and 70's were, I'm afraid, probably not much different to Brian's. This I'll qualify by saying that Dad, our dad, fought as a young man in the Korean War. He was a Prisoner of War and I can only assume that the young man who went to fight for King and Country was not the same man that came back. He was pensioned out almost right after his return and in my mind never worked again.

My childhood was a sheltered one and my upbringing down to my mother. Dad had an allotment for years and would go there, I think, on a daily basis. I went maybe three times to see him as a teenager and it was like watching a peasant farmer with his hoe. Whatever happened in Korea did for him. At home it was quiet; and any abrupt noises would elicit a rabbit in the headlights stare. It was like walking on egg shells. But hey the sixties were swinging right?! Not in our house.

I probably can't tell you much more, certainly not to help Brian but a couple of things happened to me. I was very young when Vietnam kicked off but by 1975 when it was ending we had a black and white TV and my dad went into what I can only call full prepper mode. Is that actually a thing in England? Over here it's a massive industry. The allotment shed was becoming a bomb shelter and throughout my later teens Dad was preparing for Armageddon. Any little thing or big thing. There were riots in Leeds in 1975, you know and when the Pistols started swearing on the Grundy Show it was like a satanic crime against humanity. I feel sorry in a profound way that in that era there was so little support in terms of counselling for trauma treatment. My dad had PTSD for all his adult life and his only reward, if you could call it that, was that he never worked again and had a wife and two children who he couldn't talk to or play with.

Anyway, something happened around then. My best friend from school asked me to be best man at his wedding. Like I was equipped myself, for a thing like that! Speeches, public speaking, taking the Stag away, what did I know about all that? I spoke to Mum who said *just do it quietly* and so I went out and hired a suit; only for me to be that chain's millionth customer. What joy! The reward was a limousine ride home and its use at the wedding, a thousand pounds, a case of Champagne, a weekend break for two in a four star hotel and a full page spread in the regional paper. I mean, this was in 1978. You could nearly buy a house for that thousand pounds.

By the third day the press were all over the house, and I was being asked to predict the Christmas number one which, incidentally, I did. Mum suggested to me that Dad was not coping well with this and that she thought he had actually gone missing. They found him later that day in his shed, barricaded in. They called in the army doctors to talk/tranquilize him out. I made the decision, rightly I thought at the time, to leave and so I did. I packed up a suitcase and the money, gave the rest of the winnings to my friend, apologised and hid in London for a couple of years. That's it really.

I'm living in the States, in the sun and working on a movie based on a television series I piloted based on the whole millionth customer shenanigans. For years I kept running away until I realised, after some expensive therapy that this wasn't my fault. It was never Brian's either. I often wonder if Brian was conceived because he was a replacement for me having disappeared from their lives. The last contact I had was with my mother who let me know that she would leave, with my consent, everything to Brian when she died. I obviously had no issue with this; and yes I'm aware that my only living relative apart from my daughter is thousands of miles away. Please keep me informed with what is happening to him. I'll make contact with him but obviously after these traumatic events are behind him.

Once again, thanks for your concern.

Kind regards and best wishes,

Donny Ball.

So that was that, no light could be shed on Brian's school, friends or anything really, other than if it mirrored his older brother's then it was going to be quiet; like library quiet.

In view of this latest communication I think it would be a good idea to see Brian and let him know what the score is and in less than half an hour I'm sitting with him at the halfway house. I tell him I've had an email from his brother and that his library colleagues say hello and they'll visit him soon. It feels like the brother news elicits a spark from Brian but the colleague news seems to quell it. Weird. I read an abridged version of the brother email and somewhere Brian seems to be mentally flicking through his scrap book that I do/don't have.

I realise I haven't eaten and look around for Tim.

'Do you mind if I get a pizza for me and Brian to share?' I ask when I find him.

'Not a problem.'

I order a pizza for delivery, paying the extra charge for ordering fuck all. I tell Brian that a pizza is on its way, even though I know that he's eaten and there it is again, that flicker of recognition, a shoot of life, spirit.

I spend the time it takes for the pizza to come to talk Brian through what stuff I've been doing on his behalf and how we, as a department, are trying to ensure that we make as much of his life as normal as we can. I think he's listening but he's definitely on pizza watch.

We spend an hour and a half together and Tim, having carried in the pizza and a couple of plates, leaves me to feed Brian which I happily do, explaining all the while the modifications that I'll be authorising on his behalf. I look at Brian as he's biting the last of his slice and as I look him in the eyes I detect the faintest shrug of a shoulder. Not a big theatrical shrug but a tipping of the head and a tiny lift of the right shoulder. It almost didn't happen and for now I'm not telling anyone that it did. Instead I stay another twenty minutes and get up and tell Brian that I'm glad he's getting along okay. I say my goodnights to Tim and the rest of the residents and get myself home.

At this point I'm really keen to see the famous allotment/bomb shelter but the weather is cold and miserable and now it's getting dark too. Night in for me tonight I think, to catch up on my survival game and see if I can get past level 1,300 on Cubescapes.

FRIDAY 10th November.

Today starts with a big piece of news, such big news that I pull over to the newsagents and run in to get a copy of the city paper. It's splashed across the scoop board as,

NEWS JUST IN

COURT FOR BUS ATTACK PAIR

VICTIM NAMED

Two youths arrested in connection with the attempted murder of Mr. Brian Ball, 36, on Friday 8th September have been charged and are due to appear at Leeds Crown court on Friday 17th November. The two couldn't originally be named for legal reasons due to the age of one of them.

Well that's just bullshit, I think. However it goes on,

The pair can now be committed to court following an earlier Magistrate's hearing. One of the

accused is named as 18 year old Luke Rashton. The other defendant is under 18. This case has been held up by the CPS until the outcome of the inquest into the death of a bus driver in August (see page 5).

That's it. I'm puzzled about this link and wonder if there's such a thing as a serial bus killer. Holding the tabloid out with straight arms I fold along to page 5 where, halfway down, is the Bus Driver report.

Inquest into the death of Michael Ryan Hapless, 46

Apt surname, I think.

The inquest into the bus crash where the driver died on Thursday 31st August described how he had picked up the number 39 from the bus garage and started his timetable. He had fifteen minutes to check the roadworthiness of the vehicle. Nothing out of the ordinary so he set off. No passengers had got on as he'd set off from the bus garage and not directly from the bus station. The Out of Service sign would have been displayed until the route began at his first stop. The first stop was three quarters of a mile from the bus depot at eight minutes after five in the morning. He was on time and the float was exact. There were no faults found on the vehicle, which was a Scania, built in Blackburn in 1989. The weather was normal and the roads were dry.

Prior to his first stop the bus had rounded a corner of the road, tree-lined on one side and walled on the other, with a pavement and some properties under development on the driver's near side. It was at this point that the bus driver had lost control, careered into scaffolding and been decapitated. The bus continued into the development at speed before crashing. The scaffolding poles had effectively opened the bus up like a corned beef tin peeled open with its key. Windows down the length of the bus were smashed and luckily nobody else was on board the bus. Questions from the Coroner Justice Samuels included ones with regard to cameras. Were speed cameras available? Traffic control and ANPR cameras? The response was negative given that the authority was relocating them to busier roads in line with the pollution charging lanes being brought in. The Coroner corrected the Highways Department stating that this was being reversed. Nevertheless, the cameras weren't there. Also on the subject of cameras he wanted to see for instance, footage showing that the bus was empty. Was there a dashboard mounted camera? Was there a tachometer showing speeds? All these came back sadly as negative. The representative of the bus company apologised for this but expanded on the reasons why, stating the recent increase in demand for public transport, citing the pollution lane surcharge. This had meant that old fleet stock had not been removed and what had actually happened in the case of the number 39 was that it was only in use during the days. They then switched over in the evenings to the more security heavy buses. As an aside, Justice Samuels asked whether, in relation to the latest incident, a more security focused bus might have prevented the injury caused to a... the judge paused whilst looking through some other papers, before looking up and saying,

'Mr. Ball.'

The response was no, the bus Mr. Ball was on was one of the newer ones and had all of that on it.

The road was closed for the rest of the day as the emergency services cleared up and the structural integrity of the development was established. The scaffolding company was instructed as a matter of course to take down and rebuild its structure but they said it wasn't theirs as they'd sold it to the developers. There was some confusion in the Coroner's until a fax arrived. The Coroner stopped the inquest at this point and said that the fax was an outmoded piece of apparatus and the court would only accept a jpeg. This duly arrived saying that the company helped developers with a simple three-part rule of thumb.

> ➢ Is your development fifteen feet high or more?

> ➢ Is your development going to take more than three months?

> ➢ Are you skilled enough to erect it yourself?

If the answer was yes to these three it was cheaper to buy it than rent it. Simple enough; the builders had previously bought the poles and perhaps should have removed the scaffolding firm's stickers from them. The pole's dimensions were quoted and the Coroner said that, in a nutshell, that was the weapon. The Coroner had invited the building firm in and they denied any blame. Mrs. Hapless was present throughout the inquest and was asked by Justice whether she was aware of Mr. Hapless having had any ongoing medical conditions, to which she had replied no. A toxicology report was provided from the earlier autopsy which came back negative for drugs or alcohol. In the end the Coroner concluded that the cause of death was most likely human error, adding that this shouldn't affect compensation or insurance settlements.

I spend the morning in the office ready for more cases. I see Mo and excitedly tell her that there's movement on the Brian accident. Mo looks under pressure and Geraldine looks under it too. There's a tension, an edge, in the office that I'm picking up, not a good vibe. I tell Mo that I'm off to investigate the allotment this afternoon and Mo barely acknowledges this. I slink off at lunch, same sandwich again, on white if I beat the rush.

FRIDAY 10th November. Allotment.

It's not strictly work related but I've parked the car on a side street five minutes away, wheel locked, aerial down and I'm heading to Brian's dad's. I have a photocopied plan. Each plot is measured out with a surname but climatically this is not as nice as Paris. A mist has started to descend and it's getting chilly. The track I'm walking on is made out of a line of thin gravel in-between two wheel tracks. The grass is pressed down and I can see where a car has gone over it, not rutted, not enough traffic. It isn't like the cemetery in Paris as there isn't any room to walk between the plots. Every bit of spare land has been used and it's a lot more shanty town than I'd imagined. I don't know, frankly, what I was expecting. A more orderly arrangement of sheds and huts maybe? Well this has poly tunnels, cloches, a sprinkling of greenhouses with some missing panes of glass, a couple of home-fashioned scarecrows looking forlorn and a shedload of coloured sheds and huts. There's a rainbow of whatever the cheapest paint was at any given point, nearly all tempered by the weather to give a pastel effect. Padlocks on most. Garden canes look like the only things growing as I walk up to Brian's dad's allotment. A man, probably my age, is digging away.

'Aye up,' I say, getting the hang of my Yorkshire language skills and wondering at what point I could comfortably call another man love.

'Aye up.'

'You just got this recently, am I right?'

'You the council?'

'Err no.'

'Off you fuck then.'

'Sorry, I'm not the council but I work for the bloke whose dad had this plot before you. Mr. Ball,' I say.

'Right.'

'You growing much?'

'Are you kidding, it's November.'

'His neighbours say he used to come home with quite a bit of veg.'

'Not from here he didn't, it's all stones and gravel, barely any soil, look.' and he reaches down and grabs a handful to show me.

'Looks like soil,' I say.

'That's because it is. I've 'ad to put down twenty bags of

compost. More like a building site than an allotment the amount of aggregate I've had to remove.' He went on, 'I've been waiting eight years for a patch. My dad's is over there and that's my uncle's.'

He points to two spots then points to another man and says,

'Bob's been here a long time. Ask him if owt grew here.' At this he turns away and goes into the shed.

Off I fuck, a bit intrigued and follow his pointed finger to Bob.

'Excuse me, you Bob?'

'Aye who wants to know?'

I explain again and Bob tells me over a shared flask of sweet tea that he didn't know much about Plot 94. A man who was young but acted old came and went more than most, he says; three, sometimes four times a week. I ask if much grew and Bob says not. He says the man cut a sorry figure and didn't really communicate with anyone on the allotment. Nothing wrong in that, apparently there are quite a lot of loners who come here. Bob had guessed, over time that Plot 94 and its custodian would flower so to speak, but no.

'Did that young fuckwit tell you that nothing was growing?' Bob asks, pointing at the newest occupant of plot 94.

'Yes,' I reply.

'He'll grow nothing there either,' says Bob, 'he needs to get the broad beans in now, and garlic. And peas under a cold-frame.'

Bob goes on then to say how some of the other patch holders put their surplus veg outside the man's shed and it would all go. But to see him hoe, he was going through the motions. There was no gusto in him, Bob says.

'Sad really,' says Bob 'he'd nod at you if you nodded first, he'd sit in his shed and he'd take your offerings and then he stopped. Nobody touched his stuff for a number of years which was fine as it was a barren plot. Finally it must have been his widow Dorothy who came up to sit and read and do any weeding, not that it needed any; once a week she'd walk up, spend an hour or so. Then she stopped and the Parks manager wrapped it up.'

I thank Bob for the tea and say cheerio. I set off back down the track and whilst walking and looking at my plot map the penny drops. Brian's dad wasn't turning his shed into a bomb shelter like Donald his brother had said. He'd actually excavated his own filled-in cellar to make that into a shelter. The only way to remove the rubble from the house was to transport it himself to the allotment. A great escape and that's why he looked grey, because of the dust from his own digging. Nothing grew here because of the amount of aggregate in the soil. He was just hoeing it in. I don't feel anything about this discovery if you can call it that. I've nobody to tell or confide in. It feels like I've been handed a clue or a piece of an Einstein riddle: Number 94 is a shed, number 29 is a fall out shelter. It's Friday which is a night I don't go out.

Happy now, I pop my Terrence ration on.

I Blame Terrence Episode 4

This episode starts with Terrence still in his false beard.

This is a neat thirty minute episode in that Terrence is filmed making stuff. So it's like a long MTV video show, loads of grunge but leaning to the sharper tones of today. All the while a *do not disturb* sign is metaphorically thrown around the house and garage, and it's almost like the country is waiting with bated breath for Terrence to lead them to the Promised Land. The suspense or expectation is palpable as we see Terrence moulding the Icelandic volcano pumice into tiny moulds and hours later removing them from a kiln as a small grey button. Dozens are made. The sewing machine is in full swing and acres of denim are cut out and made into clothes. These finished clothes are all individually numbered and a hand-drawn label is sewn onto each. It looks a bit like a lumberjack shirt. Hell, it looks a lot like a lumberjack shirt and yet you know that these new clothes for the Emperor are going to cost an eye-watering amount. You know that when people buy one, an original one of only five hundred made (at least in this colour) that Terrence has created an army; an army that has paid him millions and millions of dollars to look like twats. It's an okay episode but feels a little lighter that the others. I guess that's the difficulty with maintaining such an intense comedy series. Probably best that the light shows sit in the middle. I'm already hooked on seeing it through to the end. Next week's preview episode has Terrence turn his hand to brewing beer. The end credits roll.

I idly pick up a notebook of Brian's and flicking through see that Tuesday 11th July is a date boldly written in. There are quite a number of figures, not mathematical,   not decimal, more like imperial feet and inches, circled initial letter A, then RH4200? Also what I think are Dewey decimal numbers. There are a number of engineering diagrams showing numerous pulleys and figures but three words on a page give me the fear. Brian has written in capitals.

I'M WATCHING YOU.

I actually look behind me. It's as though I can feel his presence in the room whilst I'm unprofessionally going through his personal notes. Quickly I turn the page and then another - mainly blanks. This next one is a blank page apart from one word: Gotcha and the number 19 with three exclamation marks,

Gotcha 19!!!

I turn this page over and see he's recreated the drawing pin diagram from his earlier book but this one has a circled initial B next to it.

Shit causes sepsis, this'll get you, you fuck...

I'm too tired to take this in really and shuffle off to the dent that I'm going to occupy for the next eight hours.

SATURDAY 11th November. In the artisanal café.

It's Armistice Day and I hear the radio commentator mention Korea as an almost forgotten war. Well I've remembered it or just been made aware of it, I think as I pop some bread under the grill. In view of what Mo said to me I've decided to break out from my shit cooking rut and I've decided to make raclette today; an Alps dish of salad, new potatoes, gherkins and melted cheese and ham for my tea. That's a quick run into town for the ingredients and a lazy cold weekend on the couch. I really enjoy the picnic style of eating and wonder if it'd work here with a blanket on the lounge floor, bottle of plonk to wash it down. This gets me onto the whole melted cheese thing again, and I think fondue, croque-monsieur, the pizza the other night, the nachos. Could cheese be the cause of my odd Brian dreams? I'm in and out of town in less than an hour and the bus disgorges me opposite the parade from where I walk home. It's equidistant to mine and Brian's and I wonder if he'll be wheeled there by his care workers and whether it was in the bottle shop where he shouted his abuse about the jam jar.

As it is, it's put me in mind to try this artisan place because of the, quite frankly, awful customer service I'd had in the bottle bar and the vegan restaurant. I'm down the stairs of the flat and out of the door in ten minutes and walking up to the shops. There are lots of people out today and the traffic is getting louder as I hit the trinity of bottle, vegan and artisan outlets. The bistro has a sign that says Artisan Bistro. If it has to tell or yell at me what it is I immediately get that feeling of dread. I push against a door sign that yells PUSH and go in. As I make my way to the counter I'm palmed off by a perfunctory arm that indicates I should sit somewhere and I'll be served. There's one other person in. I sit myself down with a nod to the other occupant and together we listen to the coffee machine spewing out a hot milky drink. The server carries it to him, the only other person in the room, and then turns to me.

'Yes buddy, what can I get you?'

'Ermm have you got a drinks menu?'

This is a mistake. I'm handed a stack of menus somewhat larger than Brian's case notes with what the artisanal café sells. Menus for breakfast which stops at 11.45 prompt; then lunchtime service 12 until 2.45; then evening. There's a full list of breads that they make on site from spelt, emmer and bran, a full drinks menu and a Specials menu which explains that to see today's specials I need to look at the Specials board on the wall by my head. I just ask for a pot of Yorkshire tea from the drinks menu. The other occupant of this room shrugs at me like that was a repeat of the treatment he'd had. While waiting for my drink I turn to look at the Specials board and can't grasp what one of the dishes is. It's a black plastic board with holes all over and then pegged white letters are inserted to spell out the names of the specials. I'm fine with

SOUP (SEE SPECIALS) 5

Though that's directed me back to the Specials menu which says I need to see the board. I'm good with

HOMEMADE BEANS ON CHOICE OF TOAST 5

But I'm having an issue with the one that says

FIORELLE (VG) 8

The pound sign is absent on all the prices just a mix of 4, 8, 6, 5.5. As my drink arrives I ask the guy what Fiorelle is and he says,

'Little flowers mate. Salad of crocus, chickweed and meadow-foraged flowers.' Then he adds 'vegan, vegetarian, gluten and dairy-free. VG covers all that,' and then he says 'Pal.'

'Oh I knew what Fior meant,' I said, 'but I don't get the -elle bit. Doesn't that mean she?'

I'd worked in Italy and the chef-patron there had a daughter and he'd say *Piccolo fiore* all the time to her and that meant little flower.

'Mate, I've just graduated in Italian studies and like all the suffixed loaned French derivatives you can put -ella on the end of words, singular, or -elle to pluralise it,' he said with a borderline-hostile tone.

'Fine, whatever,' I say, still smarting at his rebuff and staring at

FIORELLE (VG) 8

My non-Italian tea tastes quite lovely and I contemplate Brian and how he'd fight back against such slights.

After a couple of minutes checking I realise that that are twenty covers over five tables. Five tables of four. The chair I'm sat on is different to the other three at the table, as is the laid-out cutlery. So, my fork matches a fork at the table two away and the knife with the table three away. Rechecking, it's apparent that the random look of the café's furniture is anything but. The permutations of somebody randomising the chairs, cutlery, sugar bowls and salt and pepper pots makes my head ache. Five sets of four chairs but one of each at each table, five knives but only one of each type at each table. The teapot I have matches nothing I can see on the shelf. It's beyond my comprehension how someone could go to this extreme level of effort to make the place appear quirky. Mattress obsessed I may be, but if someone with full blown OCD came in here they'd go insane in seconds.

The other occupant has folded his paper under his arm and gone; the Italian graduate has gone into the back room.

I'm on my own for a couple of minutes as I finish my drink. I leave my chair and have another look at his white peg lettered Specials board. Two minutes later his precious Fiorelle has become,

LEG OF LIVER)) 8

SUNDAY 12th November. Brian's house.

It's early afternoon and I'm sitting with Brian, his four halfway-housemates, Tim, the other giant, and Sally the cook; finishing off the Sunday lunch she'd cooked.

I'd called on the phone earlier to ask how Brian was and had been invited for roast beef and Yorkshires that I couldn't turn down. Brian and his gang are having pudding but I'm too full and just get coffee.

Tim, Sally and the other giant are talking about the Christmas party and then Tim says,

'If you're still working with Brian how'd you like to come to our Christmas party, December the eighth?'

'I'd love to,' I reply looking at Brian. There's no response.

The TV is on in the corner and the sound is off but anyone watching can see the highlights of Remembrance Day at the Cenotaph.

I'm annoyed at the office for trying to almost bully me off this case and ask Tim if I can take Brian out in his wheelchair. After a bit of a discussion between the staff I'm wheeling Brian down the path and towards the parade.

'Funny this Brian but I was only wondering yesterday whether anybody brought you down here and here we are.' I'm happy to be talking to Brian and just filling any gaps with idle chatter. I'd been thinking that our conversations were a bit 'uneven' recently, shall we say.

'I see that the court case is set for this Friday.' Nothing.

'I think I've been barred by one of these wankers this week,' I say as we near the parade, with an angry shunt on the chair. Nothing from Brian.

'Hopefully your house will be done by the New Year, Brian,' I say to no response.

We wheel past the shops and I turn him around and set off back.

'I found the cellar. Is anyone else living in the house with you?'

I walk around the chair, almost kneel in front of him and repeat the question. I get a response. It's not big but it's a shake of the head, in as much as it can be. From an immobile object any deliberate movement is mammoth. It's a no: Brian lives on his own. It's his drugs, it's his booze, his cellar.

'It's alright, Brian,' I say 'I'm not saying anything to anybody.'

I'm angry that I could be pulled away any minute from my case, when in fact I'm doing what I believe I was employed to do all along, building a relationship with and guiding this guy who, let's not forget, has nobody this side of the Atlantic who can act in his interests. I tell him I'd even like to go out for a beer with him, saying I think it would be a right laugh. Brian's arm spasms a bit and beckons as though he wants to see me face to face. I get back round in front of him and get my face level with his. With as much effort as he used when trying to say his surname as Bottle he looks at me and whispers,

'A Karma.'

'What?'

'A Karma.'

'You mean what comes around goes around?' I respond, 'I suppose it does my friend. I suppose it does.' I take hold of his wheelchair and push on back to his.

MONDAY 13ᵗʰ November.

Following the Inquest.

This is falling into place now. I can see that the bus driver inquest was heard first to see if it was linked in any way with the attack on Brian. I guess if it was proved to be foul play then the police might have been able to charge the defendants with a pair of attacks. Now that the inquest into the death of the bus driver is over, the case against the two accused in the Brian Ball case starts.

Although they were originally charged with attempted murder this has been reduced to Grievous Bodily Harm by the CPS. GBH with intent or, as it says in the paper, S18OAPA 1861. The prosecution goes on to say that it will prove beyond any reasonable doubt that the two accused, maliciously and with intent, selected a weapon or adapted an article to be used as a weapon, with the intention of causing wounding or grievous bodily harm; the adapted weapon being a four metre long scaffolding pole. The paper's court correspondent attempts to explain the reduced charge by saying that unlike murder, which requires an intention to kill or cause GBH, attempted murder is harder to prove as it requires evidence of intention to solely kill and nothing else. The judge has lifted the press ban and Rashton's co-accused is his younger brother. The prosecution say they'll provide CCTV as part of their case. The defence team are sticking with the argument that the two accused had nothing to do with anything. The trial is expected to last a week.

I pop into the office where I'm handed some post by Geraldine. I've received a Letter without Prejudice from the Ball family's solicitor, basically telling me nothing other than that the solicitor is now applying for living Power of Attorney for Brian. He won't get it because we, the State, have it. He's trying it on to give himself another gig with the family. According to our Director, the State has taken over Brian's welfare. I'd written to ask them whether Dorothy had left a will and whether Donny was included. Would whoever was executor, administer any fund that Brian would have towards his future care? I figured that a Trust of some description would be needed to actually manage Brian's finances, compensation and insurance. I knew that financing Brian's care would probably incorporate a three person team rotating at his home. This was, ballpark, £75,000 a year. Add inflation and what have you and Brian's fund, notwithstanding any inheritance or redundancy, was going to splash around the three million mark. That's if he remained in the same state as he was now. I ask Geraldine to reply to the solicitor to ask for a meeting to discuss Brian's current predicament. *Thanks again to our Director* I thought, as yet again I'd been castigated for trying to help Brian, yet this whole joined-up help method hasn't been communicated to the rest of the world.

There's a letter from the medical trauma team who have also told me to back off from asking what Brian's state currently leaves him able, or unable, to do. On the back of these knock-backs I phone Mo and arrange to see her over coffee.

So far I've been told that this department can access whatever information we require from multiple agencies only for them to refuse me every step of the way. I'm agitated by this as I now want to see some resolution to the process. I ask Geraldine if she can get me the contact details of quantity surveyors so that I can get some building quotes.

Geraldine snaps, completely snaps, scrapes the chair back, and doesn't run but walks purposefully to Mo's office, then without knocking, walks in.

A long hour later it's me sat in Mo's office, with a coffee in my hand.

'Geraldine's gone home for the day. It's not you that caused this.'

'I didn't say anything Mo, just asked her for some email addresses.'

'Have you finished your case yet?' Mo asks.

'What do you mean?' I ask.

'Can you move it on?'

'Not really Mo, I'm on leave. I've got to take some days off this week.'

She looks at me like I'm lying.

'You said it to the team, all of us. That we had to take so many days off per quarter, so that we weren't all off in February or March remember?'

Mo remembers and smiles as though it was one of the most caring and morale-boosting things she's done in a while.

'Can you pass your file onto someone? Rachel?' she asks. It's my turn to react and I wonder why I've bothered investing any time in this, but I fight.

'No! I said it'd be after Christmas. I'm getting quotes from the surveyors, I've got knocked back by the medical team and I'm in a bit of a row with the solicitor. He's trying to bully me, I think, into letting him take on Brian's welfare, but he can't because we're in charge. We have Power of Attorney,"

Mo blows out her lips, and I instinctively know but still ask,

'We do, don't we?'

'Look Simon, we're operating under an umbrella provided for

us by the DWP and up to a point we can do almost anything as long as we don't break cover or get the press involved too much. It's okay to get some publicity but stirring things up and ruffling other departments' feathers won't go well for us.'

'Shit,' I say 'don't we even care about our cases then?! What do you want me to do? Replicate what Brian has in his care home, in his own home, throw a care team in and walk away, knowing that we're taking all his money too?!'

'Can you? Is that possible?' Mo asks.

'Bloody hell, Mo! When I started it was to make a difference, this isn't making a difference, it's robbery by the State. That's not holistic it's Hell-istic!'

Mo's staring at me now as if she's waiting for me to provide an answer, which I think I do.

'Okay, let's scrap the quantity surveyors and all that and get quotes from local firms to bid for the job. I know what needs doing, I think.'

Mo nods.

'We can recover whatever money it costs when Brian's money comes through - if it ever does. Is that what we need to do?'

Mo nods again and confirms that's exactly what we should do. At this point I realise that it's not me who's out of their depth but Mo. Helping people with the rewiring of their mentals but unable to rewire a plug.

'Look Simon, I've been doing this…' she can't say it, it's

destroying her, but she does finally say it 'job,' and then adds 'this whole thing's a mess. I'm under pressure to conveyor-belt these processes along at a right clippety-clop. Don't you know why?'

'Nope.'

'Culpability. You spend three days or a week and pass it along, that's what I've been told to instruct my team to do. You can't be blamed if you've only been partially exposed to potential mistakes.'

'No pressure there then, boss,' I say, thinking that if anything goes tits up the person making the decision is toast.

Mo tries to tell me, unconvincingly, that it's the exact opposite and that we need to treat it like a game of pass the parcel. When the music stops the person with the parcel drops it on the ground, simple.

'Wow, I'm pretty sure that I didn't sign up for this, Mo,' I say, 'I thought I was supposed to build a relationship with my client, not sweep him away when I completed the home survey.'

Mo sits there. She's almost beaten but manages a big non-teary sigh and starts again, a reset, count to ten. Accept the old system works and try to circumvent the powers that be to make this a coherent assembly line of delivered care.

'What needs to happen,' Mo starts to say but can't carry on. She just sits at the desk and stares out at the city skyline; already the day has had enough and is retreating into the dark. Grey streaks are knitting their way through her darker hair and it's the first time I've seen some vulnerability. I'd only seen her as a symbol of strength up to now. Knackered is a word that would accurately describe her at her desk. Physically and mentally defeated with the conflict in her head. Toe the line, or fight the idiots above and lose anyway. I try to work through some response, some help.

'What I can see is that Geraldine's been given the role of administrator, but all of the case workers are using her as their own personal assistant,' I say.

Mo looks at me as though I've given up some revelation but it's merely common sense.

'What if,' I say 'we have a meeting and sort out which work we do and which we give to Geraldine?'

'Arrange it,' says a faraway Mo.

'You okay?'

'Tired. I'm not an office wonk,' says Mo. 'Sort out this meeting and while you're at it arrange a team night out, give us all a morale boost,' she adds. I don't know it at the time but I'll do neither of these things.

'Sure.'

I get up and leave, having resolved none of the agenda items I needed to address. I walk past Parks and Recreations and pick up the local Business Pages thinking about the three quotes for Brian's house. On the way out of the building I see another case worker, Todd I think, and ask,

'How's tricks?'

'Haven't a clue,' he says.

'What, you or them?'

'Both.'

'Boss has told me to organise a staff night out. Any particular night best for you?'

'Any.'

I leave and find my car undamaged.

In the artisanal bistro.

I'm back in here and I hope that the owner/Italian graduate doesn't notice me but he does and says,

'Very funny, messing around with my boards. Don't.'

Funny, because I see he's just finished writing a selection of beers available on a blackboard. Tea duly delivered, I sit with my phone scrolling through crap, daring to see if I can beat level 1,300 of Cubescapes. I can't and have a quick go on Survive but I can't progress on that either. Staring out at the artery of the commute all I see are tired faces on buses and in cars. It's drizzling again.

Thinking about Brian, I've used the shared tablet to email three builders and ask for three tenders for the specified work I want done. I've told them it's urgent and I guess as it's not outdoor building work, the weather should suit a quick in-out job, couple of weeks. Told them where the keys are and what our rapid payment scheme is. That should jiggy them along.

But what about Brian? Can he survive in his own place? I don't even know what his toilet arrangements are and really why should I? Not my bag, I think… no I'm not even going there.

What I'm gathering from the chats with the people he'd come into contact with is that Brian had only started drinking in the last few months. He'd probably only just started smoking and more than likely had a couple of students round for a few sessions on the old blow. This came about following the death of his mum. Letting his hair down and living it up a little, though not too successfully. His brother painted a fairly bleak portrait of his own childhood and I can't help but think Brian's wouldn't have been that much different. All just very quiet on a quiet street. Too young for the eighties, though what happened then anyway? Through school and straight into the library. Almost like he'd gone from baby to adult and missed out the entire teenage world and any adolescence. I feel a bit numb at this and think what my own teenage years were like and how they contributed to the person here. His notebooks of grievances were just fanciful weren't they? I'd read them.

And then I remember this joker of an owner has written on his board and wonder again what Brian Bottle would do. As I finish my tea, I'm guessing for the last time in here, I erase just two letters from his board: an I and a C. Instead of conjuring up an image of wild yeast to the south of Brussels cultivating the open louvered slots in the fruit laden sheds, it now reads:

Belgian Lamb Beer.

I head for the door. *Shops 2 Me 0… really?! I'd say Shops 0 Me 2!*

TUESDAY 14th November.

I've arranged to meet Amy after her day-shift for a beer. It's not a date but she's going out with her housemates later and they've all arranged to meet at the pub.

'This whole millennial thing is the way of the world at the moment,' she's saying with a half of something that's red and smells of strawberries so probably isn't. I'm having a pint of Best. Best what, I don't know, but I wouldn't ask for their worst.

Amy is probably mid to late twenties and has a degree in Psychology under her belt already. She's now on this MA half gap-half research gig. I've given her my history and she's telling me exactly why I am this way.

'You don't appreciate that the word or the idea of a meritocracy has expired. It's not about whether you're good enough, it's about being followed by twenty million people on social media. Are you an influencer, Simon?' she asks me.

'Influenza maybe,' I say sat opposite her. I'm leaning back trying to appear intelligent.

'No,' she laughs 'look, no disrespect but it's like you with your job now, and you said you were a chalet maid,' she winks at me 'you're merely a facilitator not a participant.' I take a bit of umbrage at this and tell her that she's the same. She ignores this, laughs and then says,

'And it's not even that now the world can see through this fake-ness it'll stop. It won't. Now the marketing companies want mini or micro influencers. That watch you wear, is it because you like it or because the watch company gave it to you in exchange for a weekly vlog? You're an interesting subject because you're about a year too old, not totally anachronistic, you can see the wave coming but can't surf it. It's not you, Simon it's just that it's enveloped everything and everyone younger than you.'

I'm getting a bit riled at this, it's like she's comparing me to Brian who she's never met. *He's stuck further fucking back than I am*, I want to shout at her. But she goes on,

'To be truthful it's a zoo and I wouldn't be here if I could help it. Your ways are set, memories made, choices and options exercised. We, on the other hand, are trans-gendering on a weekly fuckin' basis and the gender of our peers is a hashtag. To the Millennials you're not on the same boat, you've got a degree of independence that they don't. Christ, you could join CAMRA.'

'Do you want to wind it in a bit Amy, I don't know you well enough to be slagged off, alright?'

Memo to self: find out how to join CAMRA. With Brian.

'Get this,' she shouts over the noise of the pub busying up, 'one of my course mates, well his-or-her parental units wanted to offer as much choice as possible to their surrogate and decided that even though the gender was established they'd cover all bases. A boy was going to be Andrew and a girl would've been Wendy.'

'Yeah and?' I say.

'Well,' she leans forward and shouts into my face, 'Wendrew can decide whatever they're going to be on a daily basis!' She has tears in her eyes, real piss yourself laughing tears.

'You couldn't make this shit up! Wendrew!' she cries

hysterically and I can only stare at her blankly. I can't react, or think of a response to that. This level of faux compassion mixed with toxic cynicism, is this what I've missed? I'll drink to my lucky escape.

She calms down momentarily before finally ranting,

'And our music is shit.'

She laughs out loud. Energetic is not the word, Amy is full on and my head is spinning. I'm replaying my party days and wondering if she's off her face and if so on/off what?

Her housemates come into the pub, arrive at the table and introduce themselves. After this they go to the bar and Amy tells me that a couple of them are third year medical students.

Much as I've now taken something of a disliking to the patronising Amy there's something that's been puzzling me for a couple of days and it's just reappeared in my brain's inbox on hearing the word medical. A big flag has appeared in my mind and I need their help, not hers. An opinion on something that has been gnawing away at me.

I've been getting a niggling suspicion that Brian has thought about trying to poison someone. More specifically, the bus driver who was the subject of his unsent letter to the bus company. The driver of the number 19 bus. His notebook even has a diagram to show how he would administer the poison.

'Is it easy to give somebody sepsis?' I ask the first medical student who sits down next to me, no pussy-footing around.

'Doesn't really work like that, sepsis you contract. If you're going to manufacture it you need a culture.'

'Sorry?'

'A culture. Okay, let's start with your Petri dish from school Biology class, stick a swab around the inside of your mouth and smear it in a Petri dish with some agar. Give it time and you'll have a fairly nasty bit of kit.'

'Shit on a drawing pin?' I ask.

'What?'

'If you pooed on a drawing pin and someone cut their finger on it, isn't that going to get ya?' I ask.

'Different thing entirely, you're talking tetanus or lock-jaw. Someone healthy isn't going to suffer with that. Now the only thing is you're mistaking these two. If you're post-surgery or ill then something like the culture will wipe you out and Christ, does it and fairly quickly. As long as you're up to date with jabs well, even if you haven't had one for years the drawing pin shit method isn't going to kill you.'

'So would any toxicology report show sepsis, err... blood poisoning?'

'No, that wouldn't, it's a different test that would provide that.'

'So it would show just drugs and alcohol?'

'Pretty much.'

'Cool. Cheers for that.'

I go home, satisfied that if Brian had tried to do something like this then it wouldn't have succeeded.

Amy called me anachronistic, out of time. I'm out of step with it but surely not as bad as Brian. He's stuck, I'd hazard, at adolescence. Only in the last ten months had he restarted his teenage life. Was it the money that gave the freedom, the impending job loss, actually being free to meet people more and go out? His mid-thirties-orphaning? I couldn't answer any of these questions. There was no empathy there. I was feeling sorry enough for myself right then.

I Blame Terrence Episode 5

The opening credits appear. A Cine film all scratchy shows a small kid with Buddy Holly glasses being chased by, one can only assume, bullies; running across a grassed yard with a water sprinkler spraying a creosote-painted fence. Clearly trying to depict I guess, small town America, and then the music starts, some weird robo-folk tune with drums beating a Slaves over-dub. The credits continue with a fast forward through junior school, the boy is still running, being chased through to prep school, high school and coffee shops then white picket fences before juddering to a halt and the Cine reel rewinding back to the coffee shop. At this point three words appear as if branded onto the screen:

I Hate Terrence.

The Hate word is then erased and the word Blame replaces it.

A town sign says Anniesburg, OR, Pop 14,150.

Terrence, at his tender young age does not know how to make beer but by God he is going to make it now. With millions of dollars at his disposal Terrence buys a home brew book and having read what craft beer is made from buys the necessary ingredients. Terrence is still sporting a false beard but his real hair is growing. The programme makers show time passing with sunrise and sunset streamed for a few cycles and when we next see Terrence his hair is nearly pony-tail length. What looks like a perfectly nice home-brewed beer: see-through, pale to copper coloured, reaches Terrence's lips and he tastes it, then a rueful smile turns his lips up at the corners as he pours the liquid down the sink. The Damned, with their cover of Alone Again Or, strike up with the Mexican trumpet blaring out and Terrence has bought a purpose-built brew house and has incorporated it into a four-in-one business making coffee, speciality tea, beer and spirits. This comedy has a semi-fatalistic feel to it now and Terrence, having no shareholders or indeed anybody to answer to, is ruining everything… or so we think.

Hair thoroughly long enough for its bobble now, Terrence has the most ideal brewing process going. In come the trucks with the coffee beans and the scene pans across to a science research facility within the building, where Terrence's scientists are already looking for alternatives to coffee beans for making the coffee of tomorrow. We see bubbling test-tubes with the words flies, chia seeds and husks printed on them. The wheat and hops are also being re-purposed after their work in the brewery is done, being turned into another Terrence enterprise, Terry Vegan Crisps which is next door to Terry Brewing. The excess yeast is being put to use with all the other grains in the building making various breads and sourdoughs, that's Terry Baker. Bergamot goes into the Early Gray Double IPA 9% and Earl Grey tea – that's Terry Tea.

Beer is being distilled into whiskey, along with a small operation pickling and bottling plant, that's Terry Pickles range.

Back to the brew house and we see nibs of cocoa along with the coffee beans being ejected from their conveyor belt onto the beer making conveyor belt where they're used for making a chocolate and coffee bean porter. The process carries through to the ethanol in the distillery which marries this together for coffee gin and chocolate vodka. Genius!

Big business has a contract on Terrence that so far hasn't been executed, literally, and the adage *If you can't beat him, join him* kicks in with Big Beer producing beer that's undrinkable and making the world think it's the best thing going. Wheelbarrows of dollars are being pushed into the office, the camera pans back to a line of barrows, maybe half a mile in length, millions, billions. Once more Terrence is scuppered in his quest to destroy everything he hates and instead he wins again. Next week sees Terrence screaming into the camera. Screaming in pain. The end credits roll to a mash up of Buffalo Springsteen and Duchess by the Stranglers. That's what the credits say anyway along with the names of the actors and finally at the bottom I see: *Produced by Donny Ball.*

As has become a bit of a habit, I feed myself another morsel of Brian's notebook and I find a folded letter on the next page. I take it out and it's from the Central Library people saying they were sorry that they hadn't heard from Brian with regards to discussing the mobile library route, and in a positive move forward in concluding Brian's employment, needed the keys, petrol station card and any other paperwork returned by the fifteenth of September.

A fairly brutal letter, all in all, but having not heard from him what could they do? I look at the next page in his book and am met with a What the Fuck and an SS.

39 5.06 WTF

41 12.07 SS

0 MT

41 WTF

0 SS

39 MTW

41 TF

0 SS

39 MTW

0 TF

41 SSM

0 TW

39 T

I realise halfway down that this is actually the days of the week.

What the fuck: Wednesday Thursday Friday; a 'See You Next Tuesday' moment. Underneath this, scratched deep into the paper, is not an everyday maxim but just,

IT'S NOT THE SIZE OF THE DOG IN THE FIGHT BUT THE SIZE OF THE FIGHT IN THE DOG.

On the next page is a beautifully drawn pulley system that wouldn't look out of place in an old engineering book. Then I look again and see that it's probably been traced from one of the old engineering books from his cellar. The diagram shows the number of pulleys and where they would need to be situated in relation to each other, three in all, to lift a joist by the look of it. I wondered if this was how the cellar roof had been constructed but realise no, this looks like it was for the outside.

The next page shows a tree, it looks like an oak, which again is beautifully drawn, with various heights written next to the first and second branches. A lot of effort has gone into these tracings or free hand drawings. Something to while away his time in-between a bifter or two, I suppose.

FRIDAY 17th November.

Three days off has allowed me to catch up on life and I have a microwave oven again. Back in the office the workloads have slowed to a trickle and I haven't picked up anymore as I was on leave. Brian seems to be my only job. It looks like Geraldine's still not back and in her place is an agency typist.

I finish working on some admin for one of the other advisers and have a look online to see what happened in court today.

The court heard that Mr. Brian Ball boarded the number X19 to the Park area of Leeds from the city centre, according to the CCTV on the bus at 17.50pm on Friday 8th September. Mr. Ball sat on the upper deck two rows from the front, as the upstairs CCTV footage shows. At this point members of the jury were informed that the footage was very graphic and the public gallery saw a number of people leave. The footage continued to show a weapon, Exhibit A, crash through the window and hit the victim, Mr. Ball, in the front left side of his head. The noise caused the bus driver, Mr. Ron Logie, to look up into the upstairs seating, at the same time as performing an emergency stop. The footage continued and showed Mr. Ball being shunted backwards whilst Exhibit A seemed to try to carry on spearing his face off. The bus having stopped, the CCTV showed Mr. Logie and a number of passengers trying to save Mr. Ball.

Further outward-facing CCTV from the bus showed the moment when, from behind a high wall along the bus route, a long pole was launched, slowly at first like a cruise missile from a sub and then arrowing straight.

Further investigations found that a low-branched tree had been used as a makeshift catapult to fire the pole. Exhibit A was the four metre long scaffolding pole and the fingerprints on it matched the two defendants. Further, locally found footage showed the two defendants jogging along the path in the park from where the pole was launched and footprint analysis showed where they fired Exhibit A from.

Against this overwhelming evidence, the legal team acting for the defence changed their plea to guilty but only to the lesser charge of reckless ABH. In mitigation, the defence lawyer went on to say that they'd been under the influence. They'd been coerced by an unknown third party. They'd been self-medicating with alcohol, drugs and non-prescription medicine due to childhood traumas. They'd seen the pole and decided, for a laugh, to fire it from a pulled back tree branch with little concern for its destination. The judge remanded the guilty pair pending sentencing reports but said that they would both be going down for some time and could the parties concerned with Mr. Ball get together quickly to help rehabilitate him. The date was set for another three weeks. Bish bash bosh, all over in a day.

I pop round to see Brian to see whether the news of the case has reached them. Obviously Brian wasn't able to give evidence, but Tim tells me he was on call if needed to provide evidence of Brian's condition. In the end he submitted a document stating this for when the sentencing reports were needed.

Brian is sitting in the lounge looking out of the window as I walk in.

'Hi Brian.' Nothing. I know his hearing isn't damaged so he's probably heard Tim and me talking. 'So they got found guilty then,' I say. Nothing. I sense that Brian is holding himself back like he's playing a game. He looks at me and quietly says,

'Karma.'

'What? It's Karma that you and the bus driver were nearly killed in the same way?'

'A Karma,' he says again, a bit louder.

'The stuff I've seen in your house, Brian and the things I've read. You aren't quiet like everyone says are you? You're really cross about loads of shit aren't you?'

A barely perceptible shrug, that tiny dip of the shoulder.

'Well between you and me I'm on your side and I'm fuming.'

I get to my car and the aerial is unbroken. The car is where I left it. My mood stable, my anger level high.

Being Friday I've reserved this evening for the final episode of IBT as I've started thinking it should be called. Like BGT but not.

I Blame Terrence Episode 6

The opening credits appear. A Cine film, all scratchy, shows a small kid with Buddy Holly glasses being chased by, one can only assume, bullies; running across a grassed yard with a sprinkler spraying water onto a creosote-painted fence. Clearly trying to depict small town America, the music starts, some weird robo-folk tune with the spliced axing riff from Radiohead. The credits continue with a fast forward through junior school, the boy is still running, being chased through to prep school, high school and coffee shops then white picket fences before juddering to a halt and the Cine reel rewinding back to the coffee shop. At this point three words appear as if branded onto the screen

I Hate Terrence.

The Hate word is then erased and the word Blame replaces

it.

Kasabian's Fire hits the ears before the screen shows Terrence looking out of his office on the 16th floor of his own office block. The camera pans down and like a video game, first person walk-through we're coming into the lobby where dozens of young, hip people are milling around with their Terry coffees and going to their workspaces. Each storey, as we rise, is the same and when the camera reaches Terrence's floor we see the man himself sitting at his desk. Terrence has made his final decision, he thinks and in his multi-million dollar office he takes off his false beard and steps into his gold-plated shower. Time lapse again.

He steps forth, a long time later and dresses in his lumberjack shirt, denim jeans, leather boots and Icelandic-buttoned jacket. He steps into his private elevator to leave his tower block: Terry Towers. He exits the lift on the ground floor and is stared at by every single person in the scene. Terrence has inadvertently showered off his tattoos and forgotten to put his false beard back on. Truly the most horrific moment for a man who wanted to be the anonymous epitome of the breed he had hatefully created. He has suddenly become anathema to this species. Nobody is chucking rocks at him yet but he manages to swivel and return post-haste to his temple abode to make a few phone calls.

To the sound of robo-folk band K We Weren't There Yet, Terrence spends the next few days, according to the calendar pages counting down, screaming as the tattooist he has really employed is really tattooing him, making real all of the fake tats that he had before. Luckily he had taken a number of photographs of these otherwise he wouldn't have had a clue where they went. Half cat on left leg, geometric wheels within a feather blade on his back. A huge sleeve of tattoos on his right arm. He is also really growing a beard. But he can't grow a convincing beard and apart from the tats the very real screams are from the pain of having his face implanted, knitted and manicured with some donor's own beard. The end of this pilot series shows Terrence walking out of his self-made world with acolytes everywhere and nobody recognising him at all. A chameleon when he never wanted to be noticed in the first place.

I remember a scene from an old comedy on Gold or something where a dark haired, balding man got undressed and left his clothes on a beach and walked into the sea. It feels like that, though to a happy robo-techno soundtrack.

Terrence jumps a Greyhound completely anonymously because he's got the tats and the beard making him the same as everyone else and he kind of *Gumps* it across America for ever.

The credits roll and I have tears in my eyes, not floods just some nostalgia and what? Empathy? I decide that I'll email the producer Donald Ball tomorrow to give him an update on Brian. It has to be him.

TUESDAY 28th November.

Within my specified period to tender, ten working days, I've received the quotes from the three building firms and they only seem to confirm my theory about building contractors. One quote is massive, tens of thousands of pounds for a basic house reshuffle. Another doesn't quote enough to put you a drain pipe on the side wall and the middle one covers everything but is still overpriced by a few grand. I imagine the round robin these guys play, letting each firm get every third contract with a view to inflating their own bid for that bit extra. It's not a cynical thought but in this game it's realistic. Last week I'd told Mo that the building work would cost more that ten grand but less than eighty, it's a standard ballpark figure where we only need three quotes. I'm also led to believe from Mo that the Director himself has the authority to sign off these business expenses up to about twenty grand, without any other governing body asking why. This all feels positive yet all the while I can feel the urge from above to wipe staff out.

I feel like they're covering their backs because I'm definitely beginning to feel the heat. This is my first position in this line of work and I'd always imagined that social workers did what their names suggested and worked socially. I now see that this doesn't include working together because working together would give us power. I can't help feeling that we won't see Geraldine again. Not that I had any good relationship with her, I had no relationship with her and my clamouring for more paperwork contributed to her storming out. Nobody came to her rescue and we're all that little bit more paranoid about doing the right thing, even though the right thing only seems to emanate from our own moral compass. I start to feel a pressure on me that I haven't felt for years. Why should it be my responsibility how Brian's house ends up and not a collective goal that we agree as a group?

A division of labour, the Director would say. I'd argue that it's divide and rule. Anyway, I think I've enough experience in the rental property sector and the upshot is that Brian's house gets a second bathroom and wet-room in half of what is currently his kitchen. The other bit of kitchen and larder becomes a small kitchenette. The lounge now separates into a bedroom and a living room which also destroys his vestibule. All in all, a good sized student ground floor flat. Upstairs remains as it was apart from the box-room being turned into a kitchenette. The water run-off hijacks the water soil pipe from the bathroom, slightly off plan, and we don't plumb in another washing machine, the staff will use Brian's. The surprising thing is that all three tenders are good to go as early as we press the start button. Surprisingly, they each give a build time of two weeks. This draws a wry smile. I wonder if they're somehow related to each other, these firms. But what's it to me? I'm firmly on track now. I shuffle these bids into the case-file, jump on the spare laptop and enter this onto Brian's case notes. The best value for money will be signed off and started straight away. Mo looks glad that it's done and says,

'Let's arrange a press release on the day Brian gets back into his house. You can be pictured with him. You've done a good job, Simon.'

I realise that's it. Done a good job, finished, next. Brian; my first case and I've become attached to him in getting him the outcome we wanted. Then, puzzled, I have another look at their separate tenders and realise that not one of them has spotted the cellar.

Out of sight out of mind.

FRIDAY 8th December.

The judge, in sentencing, tells the court that the two defendants have a string of convictions; from taking without consent to aggravated burglary and assault. They've shown no remorse and in fact hadn't plead guilty at the earliest opportunity but at the last chance. The judge sends the older brother to prison for four years and gives the younger one a detention and training order for two years. It's noted by the court recorder that Mr. Ball is currently in a care facility whilst modifications are made to his home. A sympathetic judge awards Mr. Ball the most compensation that he can through the CICA; some half million for future care and physical injury.

The judge places on record the sorrow that the court feels for an innocent man going about his business who was attacked in such a life-changing way, and asserts that the sentence he's imposed should act as a deterrent to anybody thinking that antisocial behaviour of such magnitude is acceptable.

Finally the judge says that now this is settled the other parties, namely the bus company and their partners, can pay out through their insurers the monies that Mr. Ball will no doubt need to allow him to live as normal a life as is possible. Built in to this is a proviso that every two years, should Mr. Ball's condition markedly improve, the projected financial obligations will be adjusted. Any over-payment should be notified to the Compensation Recovery Unit. I'm trying to hold my phone and scroll down the page one-handed but that hand is shaking uncontrollably. These things rarely pan out to the exact amount but half a million plus the figure I'd worked out comes in at about three million.

Like, *whoa...*

The Christmas party at Brian's care home starts at seven on the day that Brian has hit the jackpot and I'm there with probably twenty other people. Sally has laid out trays upon trays of nibbles and sandwiches. The place is full, with a mix of residents and their families, case workers, staff, local councillors and me and Brian. The prosecco is flowing and everyone is enjoying themselves. I'm contemplating having to hand back the notebooks. What will I do? Quietly let myself in and pop 'em back in the drawers? Brian's barmy notes and diagrams, Brian so angry and so quiet. Why such extremes? Maybe it's down to too much fizz but I have to get out of here. I say bye and walk back to my flat.

There's an anomaly that I can't quite reconcile.

Two things hit me within half an hour. It's whilst sitting in the flat, vaping plumes of cherry blossom with can of beer in hand and head swimming, that I remember the email from Donny. Brian couldn't be angry growing up, it wasn't an option. He had to be quiet. His dad couldn't have coped with any sudden movements or cross little feet stamping. He was kept quiet.

With some sadness I pick up his book to look at the last few pages and just before I nod off in the chair I see Brian's drawing of his own bus accident; a scaffolding pole through the window at the same height as his head. The bus crashed.

SATURDAY 9th December.

I wake up physically and mentally sick and with some empty bin bags go to Brian's.

I have a hunch and as I open the cupboard in his mum's room I see the box of bedding. Lifting it out it's lighter than it should feel and I pop it on the bed and peel a corner of the tape that's sealing it. I peel it carefully down its flaps and look inside. It's neatly stacked with white cardboard boxes to nearly a third full. They have the very faded words potassium bromide and MoD stamped underneath along with instructions on how to take it. Is this what the army doctors brought to get Brian's dad out of the shed? I try to count how many there are. My mental arithmetic tells me that there are hundreds and hundreds left in a one third full box that must have held thousands. I notice that on the underside flap of the box someone else has also been doing some calculations and it says:

½ each a day, twice as long if half a day, makes the boys calmer.

This absolutely wasn't my hunch and I sit there a bit too dazed to think. I get my phone out and search for potassium bromide. I seem to think it used to be put in soldiers' tea to stop them getting the horn but I'm debunked of that myth and read that the States still use the stuff and so do vets in Germany. It looks to be a potent epilepsy drug for dogs. I imagine that back in the 70's it was a perfectly reasonable choice for the military to stockpile drugs and medicines and I think Brian's mum must have successfully appealed to the army medics to sly her a box full, saying that she wouldn't need to bother them any more if they would just do that. When Brian came along she rejigged the numbers and realised that with some husbandry she could have a less stressful home. Twenty years of PTSD for Norman and then twenty years of calm. Half each a day for her boys Norman and Brian. What did she do? Crush them up and pop the powder in their morning cups of tea?

A Karma I remember Brian saying. It wasn't the mantra I'd thought it was. It was *A Calmer* he'd wanted. How potent the drug is now, forty years down the line, I don't know but Christ, she'd hooked him and then by dying had effectively stopped his daily calmer.

I can't comprehend the full effect of this on a grieving yet emancipated mid-thirties man, an innocent addict who went cold turkey without realising it. He'd had nearly a year of freedom, doing what most teenagers do; trying to get high or drunk or both but really trying to replicate the effects of the army pills. It felt like his childhood had been erased only for him to become a thirty-six year old teenager. Everybody had said he was a very quiet man and he was, but not by choice. Who would I need to contact to report this? Certainly Mo. Definitely the Ministry of Defence. Possibly the press? Brian's mum had Norman and Brian on it for years. Half a potassium bromide a day for years. *A calmer*, she called it. It was to suppress his hormones. Used for epilepsy as well as in vets in Germany, it seems they were also given to Vets from Korea; supplied in huge quantities, years of supplies.

Then I know.

Brian has worked out which routes the driver will be on and also which buses, so as not to have the modern ultra-safe bus with loads of cameras on it. This alone was a lot of effort and then he put in even more, rigging a tree with a pulley and hoisting up an RSJ. He was against the clock because he had to relinquish control of the mobile library before October due to his job going.

I need to remove any incriminating evidence before the builders start. The pills, the drugs; even the cellar. Especially the cellar, with the models, the swinging beam, the Hayes manual showing the ride height of the bus, where the driver's head would be. The reference books, old medical books with misdiagnosed killers, old knowledge before it was updated. A brain hardwired for facts but never revisited. Football teams never changed but grounds did.

I lie down on the pocket-sprung mattress close my eyes and finally empathise with Brian.

I'm up early. I walk to the library and there I climb into the mobile and start the engine, let it idle until the temperature needle moves. A nice morning with nothing stirring. I'm raging inside but I have a quiet way about me. Years of looking and becoming still. The library isn't open for hours yet and that's okay. There, under the shelf behind the skirting, was my weapon of choice but I've gone onto plan C. I'd spent so much time making models and calculating my retribution but it had all come to nothing. Time is not on my side. I set off and imagine what could have been. Under the shelf lays a four foot long rolled steel joist that I'd found by the roadside a few weeks ago. It wasn't divine intervention but an RSJ dragged out of a skip for scrap. It was heavy too, but using the drawbridge, as I call it, I hauled it onto the van and left it there. I fully intended to hand it in, but where would I?

This was plan A. I've worked out the height of the fucker that will be wearing this as it swings with my pulley out of an oak tree's branch and, battering ram style, shatters the front of his bus and tears his limbs off. An arm for an arm. He fucked up my coat jacket and laughed; well, I'll fuck your arms up. But time is not on my side now and plan C is the solution, though I hate it that plan B didn't work…

I followed you and found out that you had an allotment with a shed and I remembered an old trick I thought of playing on my dad years ago. I never did it, I never played any tricks on him; I was a calm little boy. But you, you fuck, I spent hours filing the tack, camouflaging it, bagging it up with shit and creeping up to your spot; number 19. Can't tell if you got poisoned or not but you still turned up for work. Had to do more reconnaissance on you. Found your other route.

I've got to thank the short bloke in the pub for plan C. He was playing pool and a man twice his height tried to bully him off the table. I thought the big guy was out of order but I was a bit pissed and stoned. The little guy whacked him once with his cue and that was that, my idea. All my years of maximum effort and minimal impact. I flipped it around when I saw that, minimal effort and maximum impact.

Sun's up in an hour or so, but the light's enough to do what I want. I spend ten minutes on that side of the road, climbing out of the skylight and onto the scaffolding. I adjust the clamp and pins with a socket set. I know your exact ride height and I turn the pole and set it joust-like toward the road. No car will touch this if indeed the drivers even see it. The road is dead quiet and there's nothing coming but my bastard's bus. I pull the mobile around and position it in the bus lane. At precisely 5.08 am I see the bus and you, the driver of the bus, as you look at me, tutting and swearing and now gesticulating as you have to completely pull out of the bus lane and cross the white lines. The bus is now facing straight on to the development opposite and the protruding jousting scaffolding pole lances you. The sound of metal twisting and bricks coming down is astonishing as it shatters the silence.

I look in the offside mirror, 'Serves you fucking right you fucking prick!' I shout, fist pump, and take the mobile back to the library.

At the allotment.

Not strictly work related but I'm at the allotments. I'm not here to see Brian's dad's but I have a photocopied plan. Each plot is measured out with a surname; climatically this is not as nice as Paris but climactically it is as exciting. I was excited the other week when I was given the *must be deleted* plan of the allotments and as I read through the names of current tenants I came across a surname that I'd seen for the first and only time a few weeks earlier. Hapless. Mr. M.R. Hapless was the name that occupied plot number **19.**

I make my way up the gravelled path, past a mound of collected leaves and make out the smell of more leaves burning some way away. It's a smell I love and equate as a season starter just like the first mown grass of spring. The weather is dry and the easterly has changed to a westerly. The mild and not-yet-damp air is pleasant as I stand at the allotment site of Mr. Hapless like a mourner at a grave. I've been standing here for at least fifteen minutes and to anyone that sees me I probably look like that mourner or a prospective gardener.

I know what I'm doing; I'm empathising with a different man, who the world deemed something of a nothing, a small matter. A world that forgot to acknowledge nerve, courage and *what's the word..?*

Bottle.

The small but mighty fighter who though the process was wrong, the plan wrong, the outcome wrong, carried a heart that was fierce for revenge and justice.

My eyes are scanning the site from right to left almost imperceptibly and after twenty minutes, probably nearer ten, I move forward, bend down and pocket what I half-suspected but really just instinctively knew was here. A drawing pin filed to a thin sharp spike, painted black with model paint. I turn and walk back through the allotment, nodding a couple of times to late season gardeners.

I'm in the office along with all the other staff but Mo isn't here. The Director starts to tell us that Maureen's husband has been diagnosed with cancer and Maureen has, therefore, taken early retirement. Furthermore, the Director tells us, he's been promoted to another authority and finally there's been a change at Whitehall so the responsibility for our pilot has been handed back to Work and

Pensions. It's unlikely that any new case loads will come our way, so we're to finish the ones we're on and await our redeployment back into the mainstream.

'I don't have a mainstream, this was my only stream,' I say, hand up.

A couple of others nod but the Director reiterates that we'll be front-line social workers from now on.

It's a week later and I'm working my notice. The work on Brian's is complete and, following some to-ing and fro-ing between his brother and the solicitor and Brian, I've started a new job as his carer. I still have my flat and it still has all the evidence in it, but I'll probably sub-let it and spend more time here, there's plenty of room. The Trust, with my assistance, has successfully negotiated a care package between Brian's insurers, the bus company insurers, the CICA, the lot basically. My own contract is better than before. As I wheel him down the path to his widened door and insert the key I sense that we've seen the back of the dark nights and the days are gradually getting longer.

'Here we go then, Brian.' I push him through to his room where the bed is in the corner.

'Fancy a cup of tea or something?' I go to the opposite corner where there's a small tea-making area.

I don't hear him get out of his chair and the hairs on the back of my neck stand up when I hear the voice near my ear.

'What have you done to my fucking house?'

I turn and Brian is standing in front of me, my adrenaline

level has peaked and I'm in flight mode. Then he shrugs and with a half-smile says,

'Thanks.'

I reach out my arms and hold onto him, gently manoeuvring him back to his chair that I lower him into.

'Let's get you settled in first.'

There's no evidence in this house that any law was broken. I realise that all the evidence of these events is at mine.

I grade mattresses. This one is brand new for me, a memory foam and it feels like all the hugs I've ever had. On this I dream of Brian the murderer.

THANKS TO:

My wife Punka, who hates proof-reading my 'brain-spew'.

My daughter Evie, who inspires me every day and just

threw in the odd perfect word when I was struggling.

My sister Jane, for staying calm in the face of adversity.

Ron for constant pressure to perform and unfailing friendship.

The city of Leeds in general and in particular for just being Leeds.

The Damned, Radiohead and Kasabian for their tunes whilst writing this.

East Lancs Coachbuilders and in particular John Donoghue for speedy expertise.

Jenna never-was-a-Teapot Girl Gill.

Keith and Moz because you should have been here.

Gav and the chefs I've worked with.

Robb with a double-B.

Miles and Phil.

Printed by Amazon Italia Logistica S.r.l.
Torrazza Piemonte (TO), Italy